Lou Lou's Christmas Wish

Gunther City Mail-Order Brides Series

Book 3
2nd Edition

Lynn Donovan

Copyright

Series Introduction

August 1889, four months after the initial land run in Gunther City, Oklahoma, six men are ready to take a wife. Acting in conjunction with an affiliated church in Portland, Maine, they write a letter describing what they want in a wife.

Six women in Portland, Maine select the letter that suits them the best. Their church arranges their travels, thanks to a generous donation by a mysterious man named Nugget Nate who visited the town after a "calling" brought him to Maine. The girls board a train going to Oklahoma as mail order brides.

The six men anxiously meet the train and their new brides, except seven brides step off the train. A last-minute addition muddies the waters a bit, but the boarding house has room. Will the matches line up to be right for the couples? Can Widow Drummond keep order with so much amore in the air? Who will marry first? Only time will tell.

These are their stories.

Introduction

A woman with but one wish for Christmas: a good life with six children. A cowboy's desire for a good wife and several sons. Five orphan siblings who pray they will not be separated on the Orphan Train heading out west.

Lou Lou Lee never knew her mother. She lived in an orphanage until she was adopted, but the adoption was more of an enslavement with cruel people and a son who had evil intent for her. She agrees to become a mail-order bride and move to Oklahoma to see her dream come true.

Albert Forrest is the middle son of three who sent for a mail-order bride. His dream is to be a successful horse trainer and have a home filled with strong sons to help him run his ranch.

When parenthood doesn't seem to be God's will for the couple, Lou Lou makes a Christmas wish to receive the five orphaned children being sent to the Forrest Ranch by the matriarch's sister from New York City.

But when the children arrive, Albert's dream is crushed when they are four girls and one sickly infant boy. Can Lou Lou convince her husband that girls make good ranch helpers, especially since the oldest girl is terrified of barnyard animals and refuses to learn to ride a horse? Is there any hope for saving Lou Lou's Christmas Wish?

Prologue

Summer 1890

Hannah Jervis knew she and her son were dying. In spite of the good sister's excellent care, it was only a matter of time.

"I prayed the rosary for you this morning, dear one," Sister Bertrice removed the wet cloth from Hannah's brow. Her fever was so hot it heated the cloth in mere seconds. "May the Blessed Virgin Mary, herself, deliver you from this fever."

Hannah peeled her tongue from the roof of her mouth with a smack to lick her dry, cracked lips. Her two-month-old suckled at her breast, but with the fever, she had little for him to draw. The sister spooned broth into her mouth, which made her choke. Her throat tightened when she swallowed. Still, she urged the sister to give her more. Tipper needed something, anything, that she could get into her tummy so her baby could nurse. The sister assured her the Good Lord watched over innocent babies, but she wasn't fooled. Her son needed her to stay alive a little longer.

Her four daughters gathered at her side. Magan, the oldest, had combed their hair and tied ribbons in their red locks. She was a good substitute mother. Hannah squeezed her eyes closed. A tear oozed out and seared the side of her already moist face. She wished the sisters would take her girls outdoors and let them play, but Sister Bertrice told her the girls were anxious to be near her. She lifted a trembling hand toward them. The girls all grabbed hold and pressed their faces against the back of her hand.

"Get well, Momma," they each said. Even little Ryann said it in her own baby-talk version. At three, Hannah couldn't imagine if she fully understood that her mother was dying or that she would soon become an orphan, but Magan, at age ten, knew precisely what was happening. That was why she cried the most.

The other children in the Friendless Women's Asylum didn't help to calm Magan's fears. Hannah overheard the harsh stories the other children told her girls about being an orphan in the Roman Catholic Orphans' Asylum down the street. The children worked hard for their keep, but they received two meals a day and a bed to sleep in. The work they were expected to do was better than running the streets like so many orphans in New York City.

With every ounce of energy she had, she lifted her head and spoke to the nun who attended to her needs. "Please promise me something." She breathed the words.

The sister leaned close to her mouth so she could hear her wish. "What, dear one?"

"Promise you will put my girls on an orphan train and send them out west where they'll be adopted by a rancher. Rancher's need large families, don't they?"

"Of course," The nun patted her frail hand.

"Just—" Hannah convulsed into a coughing fit. Once she regained control she continued with a hoarseness she couldn't clear from her throat. "Just promise me they won't be split up. They need to stay together. And..." She tried to clear her throat to no avail. "If Baby Tipper survives, please make sure he stays with his sisters, so... so he'll know me and he'll know where he comes from. Magan will help him remember. She'll help them all remember."

"Save your strength, dear one." The sister touched her shoulder, then stroked her cheek. Concern filled the sister's face. Hannah knew it was the fever that gave her such an expression. She rung out the cloth in a bowl of cool water and placed it on Hannah's forehead. The cool rag soothed her brow for a moment. Hannah closed her eyes. "Promise me, on everything that is Holy, sister, promise me!"

The sister worried her lip. "You do your best to get well, and if the Lord thinks it's your time to go be with Him, then I'll do what I can to get your children out west to a good ranching family."

"Keep... together."

"Yes, dear one. I'll do my best to keep them together."

Hannah fell asleep with those words on her lips and Sister Bertrice's promise in her heart. She held on to life for two more months. But in the end, her heart just gave out.

Father Michael read Hannah her last rites and the girls gathered around their mother to kiss her goodbye. When she breathed her last, Baby Tipper began a soft, weak mewl. He barely clung to life himself. Sister Bertrice crossed herself and dropped to her knees to pray for the

children, especially Baby Tipper.

"What on earth are we going to do, sister?" Sister Madeline asked Sister Bertrice as they lifted the undersized, malnourished baby from the dead woman's body. "How are we going to keep this baby alive without his mother to nurse him?"

"The Lord will provide." Sister Beatrice said as she pulled the sheet completely over Hannah's head. "Rest in peace, dear one."

Sister Madeline turned to find four little girls, hand in hand, with tear-saturated faces, standing stoically behind her. They didn't cry aloud. Magan put out her arms, begging for her baby brother to be given to her. The sister glanced back to Sister Bertrice who nodded so slight that Sister Madeline questioned her approval. She handed the baby to his eldest sister. The four girls gathered around the youngest and sobbed into his swaddlings.

The two sisters crossed themselves and wiped tears from their eyes. They stood to wrap their arms around the children in an effort to provide what comfort they could.

"Come, let's go to the chapel and pray," Sister Bertrice offered.

The four girls staggered under the weight of their grief to follow the sisters into the wood-grained chapel and knelt at the altar. Baby Tipper inconsolably whimpered, but he didn't have the strength to cry. The two sisters knelt with them and touched their rosaries as they prayed in whispers for the Blessed Virgin Mary to provide for these so small and alone.

After a long while, the girls had cried themselves dry. The two youngest, Ryann, who was three, and Edith, five, had fallen asleep while kneeling with their heads buried in the bend of their elbows. Magan and Agnes waited for the nuns to grant them permission to stand. They gathered the baby and Ryann on their hips, lifted Edith by the arm, waking her, and made her stand. She leaned heavily against Magan. Their tummy's growled and the sisters gave each other a look, both understanding the other, that the children needed to be fed.

Entering the kitchen, they found a large crate of bananas that had been delivered that day, and a large burlap sack filled with two-day-old bread sat on the preparation table. It was a donation of surplus foods given to the nuns from the market. Sister Bertrice clapped her hand. "Praise be to the Lord."

Two other nuns stirred large pots of steaming broth with vegetables, which also had been donated from the market. Bad spots had been cut from the carrots and onions to utilize as much of the vegetables as possible for a soup to feed everyone in the asylum.

Sister Bertrice sat the girls at a small table and gave them each a banana, a slice of bread, and a bowl of the soup. Magan dipped her little finger in the soup and let Baby Tipper suck on it. He seemed lethargic at first, but his efforts became more vigorous as Magan continued to give him more. She mashed up a fourth of her banana to a smooth paste and scooped small portions into his mouth. He gummed and tongued the fruit until he swallowed. She looked up at Sister Bertrice. For the first time the sister saw hope in the girl's eyes.

"The Lord always provides," Sister Bertrice said and gave Magan another portion of soup and another banana.

Sister Madeline slipped up beside Sister Bertrice and whispered in her ear, "They'll need to be transferred to the Roman Catholic Orphans' Asylum."

"Yes, sister, I know, but not today." Sister Bertrice smiled at the girls as they tucked into their meal. She promised their mother she'd get them to a ranching family out west, and with the Lord's help, she intended to keep that promise. Tonight she would write to her own family in Oklahoma and see if her sister and brother-in-law could help.

Chapter One

Three years earlier...

"What are you doing up so early?" Lou Lou Lee squatted on a one-legged stool, milking the second of four cows. She drew her shawl tighter around her shoulders. The barn was dark and the air was cool, but that was not why she felt the need to cover herself.

Amos Lewis, the oldest son of the Coy family, slithered into the cow barn with a greasy smile that meant he was up to no good. "Came to see how my favorite sister is doing," Amos hissed.

"I'm not your— look, I've got these cows to milk and eggs to gather before I make breakfast, what do you need?" She winced for speaking so harshly to him. She wasn't allowed to speak her mind. Ever since they paid the orphanage an adoption fee, she had served the family more as a subservient worker than an adopted daughter.

Amos had lurked in the shadows, always watching her, since they brought her here two years ago. Over the last six months, with her womanly features becoming more than she could hide with the foundation garment Mother Coy gave her and a shawl, Amos had been blatantly bold in approaching her. He would corner her in isolated places, like this barn, early in the morning when the rest of the family was still asleep and couldn't hear her cry for help.

"What do you expect?" Amos licked his lips, exposing chewing-tobacco stained teeth. "You're sitting there in a most inviting position, with your ankles and shins exposed."

"I thought I was alone." She tugged at her skirts to cover her boots. Balancing on the stool while milking the cows made it difficult to remain ladylike. Exposing her legs didn't matter when she was the only one awake. Today, it mattered a great deal. Amos, of course, would take advantage of the situation and accuse her of being inappropriate. Toying with him, he had called it.

A shiver of disgust rippled down her spine. She would never... toy with him for any reason. All she wanted was to reach the legal age of seventeen and get away from these horrible people. She had two years to go.

Amos meandered among the cows who were waiting to be milked. They bawled as he walked around them, begging for relief from their taut udders. He didn't grab a stool and milk any of them. He had more malicious ideas rolling around in his head. Lou Lou watched him closely as she drew the milk, rhythmically squirting it into a wooden pail. Her gut instincts told her to get out of there. Her sense of duty told her to get the milk and gather the eggs. She had work to do and the family was counting on her.

He came around the rump of the cow she squatted beside, his elbow propped on the bovine's back hip. "You sure are turning into a purdy woman, Lou Lou."

She paused with her hand in the downward motion. The milk shot a stream into the pail, then slowed to a drip. Her eyes remained focused on her hands. Slowly, she turned her gaze to look at him. He had unbuckled his belt and continued to loosen his pants. Milk splashed onto the straw floor when she kicked the bucket over, trying to scramble to her feet and back away. He caught her shawl and pulled it from her shoulders. She let it go so she could run out of the barn. "Amos! Don't!"

"You know you want it, you been giving me lots of signs."

"I ain't given you no signs. I'm only fifteen. Amos, don't, please."

He clawed at the back of her dress, but she slipped out of his grasp and ran. She ran as fast as she could without stopping to look back. His footfall was behind her for a ways. She ran through the forested area to the east, toward town. It was the only direction she knew where she could get help. She hoped.

Amos yelled something foul at her when he stopped running. She never looked back. She ran and ran until her side hurt, but she continued to run even through the pain. Finally she saw the city, Portland, where she had come from the orphanage. She couldn't go there. They'd send her back to the Coys for sure. Since they had adopted her, legally she belonged to them.

No, she turned on Water Front Road and ran straight to the church. Her legs gave out as she tripped up the steps and collapsed on the grey painted veranda.

"Help," she breathed. Her air was spent from running.

Pastor Robertson answered her feeble call. He lifted her to her feet and brought her into the sanctuary. Through tears and fears, she told her tale and begged him not to send her back. He told her there was a place for everyone who wanted a new life in the House of God.

"I'll do anything, Pastor. I can cook and clean. I'm a hard worker, I don't need much, just a mat in a corner. I won't be no problem," she cried.

"Oh, my child, we can do better than a mat in the corner and I have an idea of a worthwhile place you can serve until you are old enough to marry," Pastor Robertson reassured her.

Pastor and Mrs. Robertson took her in and let her serve in the Community Kitchen, providing meals for the homeless and abandoned who lived on the streets. She was given a small room at the back of the church with a bed and a small dresser, much like the simple rooms the nuns had back at the orphanage. Mrs. Robertson was as kind as a loving foster mother could be. Nothing like the Coy's mother had been.

"Mrs. Robertson, I appreciate the shelter you give me here, but I'm fifteen, I should find myself a husband and stop being a burden to you and Pastor."

"No, sweet Lou Lou," Mrs. Robertson touched her callused hand. "Fifteen may be the legal age to marry, but, trust me, you are too young.

Stay with us until you're seventeen, then we'll pray and the Lord will provide you His chosen path toward marriage."

Being an orphan without real siblings or a consistent motherly figure, Lou Lou longed for a settled life. She dreamed of marrying a good man who would love her with all his heart and having a house full of children. It had been her wish all of her life. She couldn't imagine how any good man would want to take her as his wife, but Mrs. Robertson told her to pray and the Lord would provide. She believed

that with every fiber of her being. It just had to be true.

On her seventeenth birthday, she told the pastor's wife she was ready to make her own way. She had no idea how she could possibly make her way, but with their help and the Lord hearing her prayers, she would figure something out. Mrs. Robertson showed her some letters from men who lived in Oklahoma who were looking for brides.

This was the answer to her prayers. She took the stack of envelopes tied with a red ribbon, and knelt at the altar, asking for guidance. Once she thought she had spent enough time bent over the envelopes, she sat up and closed her eyes. Sliding her slender finger over the edges, she stopped where she felt she should, and pulled that letter from the bundle.

She gave the others back to Mrs. Robertson and held the one against her heart. "Let this be the one," she chanted on her way to her room. She sat on her little bed, her heart pounding with anticipation as she broke the seal. The handwriting was neatly written with ink and pen. The stationery was cream colored. There was no odor to the paper, for some reason she had thought it would have some essence of the man's scent. She giggled at her childish expectations and unfolded the letter.

"To whom it may concern,

"My name is Albert Scott Forrest. I am the middle son of Pete and Gladys Forrest of Gunther City, Oklahoma. We all participated in the Oklahoma land run last spring and each acquired one hundred and sixty acres. Being a loving family, we all work together to build a herd of cattle and other livestock for the ranch. My passion and focus on the ranch is gathering the wild mustangs from the prairie, taming them, and breaking them to be ridden by the cowboys. I hope to build a profitable business of trading ridable horses.

"I am looking for a woman who is sturdy, that is, able to have a large family (the more sons the better, but I think a few daughters would be nice, too) and work hard to help me build our ranch and horse business to a comfortable success. Currently we, my brothers, Pa, and myself, have 100 head of cattle, 30 wild mustangs (ten of which are already broke), 15 goats and two dozen chickens. My youngest brother raises prize-winning border collies that help with round ups.

"It is a good life here on the Rocking F Ranch. Although our town is only three months old, it has developed into a prosperous community and full of good, hardworking people. I look forward to sharing all of it with a loving wife of the Lord's choosing. If you feel you are that woman, please return my post and tell me about yourself.

"Truly yours,

"Mr. Albert S. Forrest"

Lou Lou leapt from her bed hugging the letter to her heart and twirling around until she was dizzy. She fell back onto her mattress. Two things in his letter rang true for her. One, he wanted a large family, and two, he sought a woman whom the Lord chose for him. That had been her wish all along. Every Christmas she wished for the good Lord to give her a good husband to love and cherish and who would love and cherish her in return. She sighed dreamily and read his letter a second time.

He was perfect! This was the one she wanted to meet. She would tell Mrs. Robertson and ask what she should do from here. Lou Lou tucked Albert's letter under her pillow and skipped out to find the pastor's wife for directions and some stationery.

Mrs. Robertson was delighted to learn Lou Lou wanted to respond to one of the letters. She held both of Lou Lou's hands in hers and prayed with her, rejoicing over her good future full of love and prosperity. She gave Lou Lou a pen and an ink bottle, then she pulled a drawer in the pastor's desk and handed her an expensive sheet of stationery. "You should write to him on this. It will let him know you mean well and are sincere. Tell him your wishes, just as you have told me, and share with him a little about yourself. You don't have to share everything, like the time you spent with the Coys, but tell him your heart's desires. In your letter to him, respond to what he told you about himself and ask if he wants to continue to correspond."

Lou Lou hung on every word of Mrs. Robertson's advice. Would he still want to correspond once he knew she was an orphan and this was her only hope for a good life, to go out west and marry a complete stranger? With those thought swirling in her mind, Lou Lou sat down at the small table in the kitchen to pen her response.

She wrote:

"Dear Mr. Albert Scott Forrest,
"My name is Lou Lou Lee."

She paused, thinking what to say before she wrote. This one piece of stationery was expensive and she did not want to have to ask Mrs. Robertson for another because she had scribbled something stupid and wanted to start over. She spoke out loud, listening to her thoughts, and then wrote the words.

"I am seventeen years old, which is the legal age of an adult in my state of Maine, but because I was raised in an orphanage, I am more mature than most girls my age. I say this to assure you I am trustworthy to take care of a home and a husband. I am a good cook. I will keep your house spotless and your clothes washed and pressed. I won't ask for much in the way of personal belongings. I am sturdy and enjoy a hard day's work.

"Your ranch sounds wonderful. I have lived most of my life in the city, but I spent a few years working for a family in the country where I learned to milk cows and tend to chickens without fear. I would love the opportunity to learn how to care for horses.

"I, too, dream of a large family. Sons and daughters sound like a worthy goal. Like you said in your letter, I have prayed the Lord would choose a good husband for me. If you feel I fit your bill, I certainly feel you fit mine.

"Please return my post should you decide I am the Lord's choice for you.

"Yours truly,

"Miss Lou Lou Lee,

"Portland, Maine."

She re-read what she'd written. Was this the stupidest response ever? She blotted the ink and lifted the stationery. She'd ask Mrs. Robertson to read it and let her know if it sounded all right.

As it was, Mrs. Robertson thought it was perfect, not having read his letter, and helped her address the envelope. She would take it to the Postmaster in the morning. Lou Lou completed her evening chores after eating dinner with the Robertsons and excused herself to retire early to her room. She wanted to read Albert's letter again before she went to sleep.

As Lou Lou lay down on her bed, she took the letter out from under her pillow, read through it again, and kissed it. "Goodnight my sweet Albert Scott Forrest."

She slipped it back under where she would lay her head. That night, she dreamed of living on a ranch, with six children clamoring at her skirts. She baked cookies and pies for their delight. Her tall, handsome husband came in from a long day's work, kissed her sweetly, tousled the children's hair, and sat down to pray before tucking into a delicious meal she had made just for him. She was happier than she could imagine.

She woke the next morning giddy as a goose on Sunday. Mrs. Robertson had delivered Lou Lou's letter before breakfast and told her if he accepted her response, she could gather her things and be ready to go to Oklahoma with other mail order brides next month.

Mrs. Robertson also told Lou Lou about the generous, but anonymous, benefactor that had been through Portland several years ago and had given them a fund to help girls like her seek a new start and a better life out west. She assured Lou Lou she would be provided for until the day she married this Mr. Albert Forrest.

The thought made her rise on tippy toes and squeeze her arms around herself. A flicker of love already sparked in her heart for this man. She just hoped he accepted her letter and asked her to come to Oklahoma to be his wife.

Chapter Two 

Nearly three weeks passed, but Albert Forrest had not written Lou Lou back. Her heart soared every time the train whistle blew, but plummeted when Mrs. Robertson reported there was not a post for her. Had he thought her too young? Too naïve? Variations of how she should have written her letter bombarded her every waking hour. If only she'd taken more time to think about what to say and had written a better letter. Her dream of living on a big ranch, taming wild horses, and raising a yard full of children was ruined by her haste. Tears soaked her pillow every night. She'd never find the man of her dreams. She might as well join the convent and become a nun. She certainly had experience living with the sisters her first thirteen years of life. It wouldn't be so bad.

Another week crawled by. Trains came through town delivering nothing for Lou Lou from Oklahoma. Her heart broke from loneliness and despair. Then one afternoon, while she was serving the noon meal to the destitute who came through their community kitchen, Mrs. Robertson rushed in, calling her name.

"Lou Lou, it came!" Mrs. Robertson panted. "You got a letter from Mr. Forrest."

Lou Lou darted her eyes down the long line of people waiting to be given a meal, and back to Mrs. Robertson. "What do I do?"

Mrs. Robertson dashed behind the serving line and untied Lou Lou's apron. She wrapped it around her own waist and shooed Lou Lou back. "I'll take care of this, you go read your letter."

Lou Lou didn't wait for anyone to say she had to stay in the serving line. She grabbed the letter and hurried to the alley where she sat on the back stoop and broke the seal.

"Dear Miss Lou Lou Lee,

"I am happy to learn that we both have the will of the Lord in mind when choosing our future mates. You have had a hard life for one who sounds as sweet as buttermilk pie. I showed your letter to my Ma and Pa, and they agree with me that you sound like a girl I would like to get to know better. I look forward to meeting you in person when the brides arrive in August. Until then, I hope we can correspond and get to know each other a little better.

"Also, I want to apologize for not writing you sooner. We took some of our cattle to market and it took me away from the ranch for a couple of weeks. When I got home, Ma showed me your letter. I hope you will forgive me for taking so long.

"So, a little about me. I am the tallest of three sons, nearly 6 feet. My pa says I have a gift with horses. That's why I have been successful at rounding up the wild mustangs and taming them down so they can be a horse that can be broken. I have developed a reputation already for having spirited, but well trained, horses, which is what is needed in these prairie lands.

"My mustangs are very intelligent animals and have learned different tasks needed to handle livestock. That's a big deal, because normally a horse is a cutter or a roper. Others are better suited for packing heavy loads, like for hunters or trappers who haul the carcasses to town for trade or processing. I'll teach you more about that when you get here.

"My point is, these mustangs are so intelligent, they learn more than one function and are excellent at both. That makes them more valuable.

"Well, I have told you a lot about horses and not so much about myself, but I guess it shows you how much my horses mean to me. And why it is important to me to have many sons.

"I look forward to hearing more about you.

"Until next time,

"Yours Truly,

"Albert S. Forrest."

Lou Lou's heart soared. He accepted her! She was going to be a rancher's wife! She sat down immediately and wrote him again, telling him how much she looked forward to working with the horses and learning more about being a rancher's wife. She expressed her reasons for wanting at least six children and how she longed to give her own children the love and security she never had.

He wrote to her again and she answered him the same day. She couldn't wait to lay eyes on this man who seemed so sweet in his letters. She just knew he would be handsome and kind. She had no doubt she

was going to be the happiest wife in the whole wide world.

Word must have gotten around that she was soon to be a mail-order bride, and she had nothing to offer the groom's family but herself, because one night, a crate with four chickens was left on the church's back steps. There was no indication who had left it, except a tag that read, "For Lou Lou Lee."

Who could have given her this kind gift? Mrs. Robertson shrugged the mystery off with the usual response from a pastor's wife. "The Lord works in mysterious ways."

"Ayah, indeed He does," Lou Lou agreed.

The next night, Amos Lewis Coy knocked on the church's back door. He was thinner and stragglier than Lou Lou remembered. Mrs. Robertson answered the knock with her usual kindness, until she realized who stood on the other side of the screen.

"You have no business here, Mr. Coy." Mrs. Robertson spoke with a sternness Lou Lou had never heard from her.

"I come to get my bride." Amos growled. "I appreciate you taking care of her until she reached a proper age for marryin', but I'm here to take her home now."

"Miss Lee is not your bride, Mr. Coy. She never promised to marry you. In fact, she ran away from you because you tried to take advantage of her innocence. Your family was cruel and treated her like a slave."

Mrs. Robertson's chin was firm as she stood up to Amos. Lou Lou ran to the pastor's study. "Pastor, come quick!"

He yanked his reading glasses from his nose. "What is it, child?"

"It's Amos Lewis Coy at your back door. Mrs. Robertson is dealing with him, but you better go. He can be vicious when he wants to be."

Pastor leapt from his chair and pulled a small key from his vest pocket. He unlocked a tall cabinet and lifted a double barrel shotgun. The pastor hurried through the sanctuary to the kitchen where Mrs. Robertson had not opened the screen to let Amos in. "What are you needing young man?"

Pastor Robertson's booming voice gave Amos Lewis pause. He stepped back from the screen and smiled. Lou Lou knew that smile. He was up to no good.

"I paid for my betrothed, fair and square. A crate of chickens for Lou Lou Lee."

Lou Lou gasped. Amos had delivered those chickens. The tag had been misunderstood. It wasn't a gift for her, but in exchange for her, a bride gift. Her stomach clinched and nausea lapped at the back of her tongue.

"Please don't make me go with him," she pleaded.

Mrs. Robertson turned with shock on her face. "Dear one, we would never make you go with anyone you didn't want to go with. He has no claim on you. Put your mind at ease."

She took Lou Lou by the shoulders and hugged her close. "Now, you go to your room. The pastor and I will handle this... gentleman."

Lou Lou glanced around Mrs. Robertson to see Amos's face. His look of defeat was priceless to her. She scrunched her nose and stuck out her tongue at him, then turned and ran to her room. She would never again have to fear Amos Lewis, or any of the Coy family for that matter.

The next morning she heard the chickens clucking in the backyard. She found Mrs. Robertson and asked why they still had the crate. Mrs. Robertson grinned a rather smug expression. "The pastor had a long talk with Mr. Coy and by the time he was through, Mr. Coy decided the chickens had been a congratulatory gift to you and he didn't need to take them back."

She giggled as if there were more to the story than that, but Lou Lou didn't press her. She decided to be grateful she had a crate of chickens to take with her. Now she wouldn't arrive in Gunther City empty handed. Besides, a ranch could always use more chickens.

Before she knew it, the other letters had been chosen by five other women. She had known them when she attended school in Portland, but hadn't seen hide nor hair of them in years. A glimmer of a thought passed through her mind. Would they remember her? She was thirteen last time she attended school.

The day before they were to leave for Oklahoma, Minnie Smith suddenly showed up on the church's front porch, desperate and scared.

Lou Lou knew exactly how that felt. There weren't time for her to choose a letter or write to a potential groom for Minnie. She would be going without a man waiting for her in Gunther City. The Robertsons suggested that sending her out west would be the best solution to her problem, whatever it was. None of the girls knew exactly what Minnie's story was. Only that she would be joining them. Lou Lou's heart ached for Minnie. She would do everything she could to be a friend to her, as soon as opportunity allowed.

Lou Lou had very little to pack, but made sure what she had was clean and pressed. Her boots were polished to a gleaming shine. It wasn't much, but it was enough. She had three day dresses, two Sunday-go-to-meeting dresses, a dressing gown, and a sleeping gown, one foundation corset, two camisoles, three pantaloons and two pairs of wool stockings. It was more than what she showed up with two years ago, and certainly enough to get her to Oklahoma. She meant it when she told Mr. Forrest she didn't need much.

She walked back to her little room to double check her belongings.

Tomorrow was the big day.

Lou Lou and her six sister brides boarded the train the next afternoon. The girls had changed so much in the four years since she lived at the orphanage, she hardly recognized them. Except for Dixie Levine. She looked the same.

Old friendships rekindled quickly. Dixie Levine and Martha Grace Dickery took Lou Lou into their fold as if no time had passed since they saw each other last. Minnie seemed so lonely and scared, Lou Lou found every opportunity to befriend her as soon as possible.

Alice Canning seemed to teeter between being snobbish like Helen Baird and sweet as cherry pie like the rest of her friends. Lou Lou remained cautious, but optimistic Alice and she would develop a close relationship. All seven of them would need each other once they got to this Gunther City. No matter how arrogant Helen and Jane Anne Taylor acted, Lou Lou tried to keep this in mind and not alienate them, regardless of their behavior.

When the train arrived in Gunther City, the girls lined up. One by one they exited and found their intended. Lou Lou and Martha Grace walked out of the train together. With their bags and baskets of food the pastors had provided, they barely fit side by side, so Lou Lou stepped ahead of Martha.

With only three gentlemen left, Albert Forrest and Deputy Andrew Ootaknih hurried toward the two brides. Lou Lou's eyes widened when the tall, dark, and muscular rancher's son held up a sign with her name written out, confirming he was her intended. She pointed at him and then to herself with a smile. He was just as she had imagined, maybe even more handsome.

The steward turned and offered a hand to both women as they stepped down. In Albert's excitement he rushed up, took hold of Lou Lou by the waist, and swung her down off the train. She squealed with delight. He was strong, too. Then she sobered and feigned modesty. In truth, she had loved his enthusiasm. It matched her own feelings.

A woman dressed in widow's weeds and another woman yelled at the same time. "ALBERT! Put her down!"

Albert glanced between the two women, flushed with red hot embarrassment, and yanked off his hat. He twisted it in his large hands. "I'm so sorry, Miss Lee. I'm just so relieved that—that you're so purdy."

Lou Lou closed her eyes and squashed the memories of Amos calling her that and his horrible intentions toward her when he said it.

The second woman yelled again, "ALBERT!"

He looked up, startled. "I mean..."

He cleared his throat and straightened to his full height. "I'm pleased to make your... um, acquaintance." He grinned so big Lou Lou thought he might burst, and he was breathing so hard, she feared he'd pass out.

Albert Scott Forrest was not Amos Lewis Coy, she told herself repeatedly and continued reminding herself she was no longer in danger. She had nothing to dread. Albert would treat her like a proper lady. Her life at the Coy's farm was behind her. Never would she have to live like that again. This Albert Forrest would help make all her wishes come true.

"Thank you, Mr. Forrest." A giggle found its way out of her heart. His enthusiasm put all of her anxieties at rest. "I'm pleased to make your acquaintance, too."

In fact, he was so handsome, the love she thought she had developed for him while anticipating this meeting doubled, maybe even tripled, once she saw him in person. Her heart leapt in her chest as she tumbled head first deeper in love with him. She could only imagine how wonderful this courtship was going to be. He extended his elbow exactly as the other men had done for the previous sister brides.

Lou Lou glanced at the woman in black under the shade of the ticket office and realized she watched their every move. She must have had some part in training these boys for the girls' arrival. Lou Lou tucked the thought away to thank her later. She must be the Widow Drummond that Mrs. Robertson had told them about and knew she would get to know her very well soon enough when they all moved into her boarding house.

Chapter Three

Lou Lou and Albert hit it off from the get go. That first night they attended the first dance, which was held out at his family's ranch. It was the three brides' first glimpse of where they would live once they married their Forrest son. Lou Lou shivered with cold memories of her life at the Coy farm. She had to constantly remind herself this was a new life and the Forrests were a completely different breed of people.

Albert sensed Lou Lou's discomfort and pulled her aside. "Miss Lee, what is bothering you? Am I doing something wrong?"

"No, Mr. Forrest, it's not you. Please forgive me. You see..."

Lou Lou and he sat on some hay bales while she slowly told him about her contrived adoption by the Coy family. How they treated her like a slave rather than a daughter and how Amos Lewis had tried to corner her in the cow barn with indecent notions.

She feared that with telling him her past, this would be her first and last opportunity to spend time with him. After he knew the realities of her life, he'd harbor feelings of disgust and ask to be released from his betrothal to her. However, Albert held her hand while she spoke. Anger burned in his eyes, but not at her.

When she finished her tale, he cleared his throat. "Well, Miss Lee, I hope you believe me when I tell you nothing will happen to you like that here. My family is a good Christian family, and Ma and Pa will love you like the daughter you will be to them, once we marry. Shoot, I think Ma is already smitten with the idea alone of having three daughters to share cooking secrets and other female matters."

A crimson hue flushed Albert's face. Lou Lou laughed and touched his arm. "Oh, Albert... may I call you Albert?"

"Please do, Lou Lou."

They both snickered at the informality.

"I've never had parents, but I've always wished for some. I love the idea of having a mother to show me how to be a good wife. Oh, Albert, I want to be the good wife you hoped for when you sent that letter for a bride." She pursed a smile. He took her hands into his. "Lou Lou, from what I can tell, you are just that."

They gazed into each other's eyes, wanting to savor this moment, but their attention had been drawn to Alice Canning who had taken down a wood saw and was on the riser with the fiddle player. The crowd had gone silent, waiting to see what she did when she made them all laugh by demanding without saying a word for the fiddle player to hand her his bow.

Lou Lou and Albert moved closer to see what Alice was up to. After she played *Amazing Grace* on the saw and everyone applauded, Lou Lou turned to Albert and explained that Alice was known back home for having so much talent at making music. "It was rumored she could make music out of any ordinary object, I guess it's true, because that performance was really something."

"She's something, alright. My brother is a lucky man to have chosen her for his bride-to-be, but I'm very happy with my choice."

Lou Lou grinned from ear to ear, and ducked her head, coyly. "Aw, Albert. You're the sweetest!" She rose on tiptoes, placed her hand on his shoulders, and kissed his cheek. His eyes rounded and he turned to look at her. "Miss Lee!"

Lou Lou started. Had she been too bold? "I-I'm sorry."

He put his hand around her waist. "I'm not." And swept her out onto the dance area. They danced the remaining of the evening, until the sheriff stood on the riser and announced it was time to take the brides home.

Albert rode with Lou Lou in the keenly decorated wagon, with small lanterns strung along the sides. He and his brothers would ride back to the ranch after escorting their intendeds into the Drummond's Bride House. They had left their horses in the Gunther Stables.

Lou Lou kissed his cheek and said goodnight. He asked her if he could take her on a picnic the next day. She agreed to go and told him goodnight one last time. He didn't turn to leave until she reached the first landing and looked back. He blew her a kiss and she hurried up to the third floor.

Her room was next to Minnie and Dixie. She was so excited to tell them all about her experience and how wonderful Albert was, but they both seemed preoccupied with their own thoughts. She dressed for bed and wrote in her diary, instead. When she finally laid her head down to sleep, she dreamed of Albert and all the beautiful children they would have, the horses running in the meadow, and being so happy she could

burst.

Everyone had her own story, her own past to put behind her. Lou Lou was no exception. While a lot of dramatic things happened to the other sister brides over the next several weeks, including a bank robbery, and Minnie Smith learning she had to go back to Portland for a few weeks, Lou Lou and Albert were quickly falling in love and very much enjoying each other's company.

They scheduled as much time together as Albert could work into his busy schedule at the ranch. He took her on picnics along the Turtle Creek and took her to the ranch numerous times. She loved watching him work with the wild mustangs. He explained how he would rope them out on the prairie and bring them together in a makeshift corral. He'd spend time out there sleeping on a bedroll next to the temporary fence. He let the horses get used to him and determined which ones were going to be good for breaking and selling and which ones he wanted to keep for the ranch. Sometimes he even let them go back to the wild herd. It was something he couldn't exactly explain, he just knew by how they reacted to his presence whether they were going to be good riding partners or not.

Albert took her out to the prairie where he had a dozen wild mustangs corralled. Ranch hands went too, so they were never improperly chaperoned. The horses were spirited and anxious when she stepped down from the horse she rode. "Oh, Albert!" she exclaimed. "They're beautiful."

Slowly she approached the temporary fence and watched as the horses darted around, rearing up above her head and running into each other.

"It's alright." She cooed to them. "My name's Lou Lou. It's alright." She began to hum softly a song she knew from church. Their frantic jutting about slowed and soon they stood still.

Albert walked up beside her and put his arm around her shoulder. "You have the gift, too."

It pleased her so much to know he was pleased with her. This was the same thing she did to calm the cows at the Coy's farm. She had no idea it would work on wild mustangs, too. She turned to gaze at him. Pride shone behind his beautiful brown and golden flecked eyes. "Do you really think I do?"

"Definitely." Albert smiled and turned to watch the horses amble around the corral at ease. One black and white mottle-faced mare came to the fence and lifted her head up and down as if greeting Lou Lou.

"Well, hello to you, too." She stepped up to the horse, placing her hand under the horse's head and nuzzling her muzzle. "Aren't you a beautiful thing. I've never seen horses with these colorings."

Albert slipped back from the two of them and let Lou Lou bond with the horse he now planned to give her. Lou Lou glanced over her shoulder as she leaned her face near the horse's head. "She's amazing."

He smiled and pulled her into his arms. He touched her wind-swept hair and pushed it out of her eyes.

Her heart tripled its beat as he held her gaze. She longed to caress his lips with hers. If only they were married, she'd be so bold as to raise up on her tippy toes and kiss him right here. Her midsection burned with desire.

"She's yours," he said.

Lou Lou's eyes widened. What had he said? She swallowed hard to regain her composure. "Oh Albert. You-you're giving her to me?"

"If you want her." He pressed her against his firm, muscular chest. She felt like warmed wax in his arms, molding against his body. He wanted to give her this beautiful beast. A gift. Just for her.

"Ayah, I do want her." Reluctant to pull away from his loving embrace, she turned to the horse and combed her fingers through the mare's mane. "I'll name you something special... let me see." She considered carefully. "You are black and white, dark and light, dusk and dawn. That's it! I'll name you Lovely Dawn."

Albert chuckled. "Lovely Dawn she shall be, then."

"When can I ride her?"

Albert laughed. "She needs to be tamed first, but I'll work on that and you can ride her as soon as I know it's safe."

Lou Lou smiled and folded back into Albert's arms. "I can't wait to get to know her better."

Albert kissed the top of her head. "It won't be long."

With each passing day, Lou Lou's love for Albert grew. So did her desire to be his wife and share her love with him in their marriage bed. A burning sensation bloomed within her whenever he held her close to his strong, taut body. She had heard about these passions from the more promiscuous girls in the orphanage, but had never imagined how it might feel to have them. Amos Lewis Coy never stirred any feelings in her heart except fear and loathing.

She knew soon she would be able to express her passions for him once they married. Until then, she would control her fervor as was expected of her, but she wished Albert would make the decision and ask her to be his wife.

She would say yes, of course. It was just a matter of him speaking the question.

He, too, expressed his affection for her in so many sweet and thoughtful ways. He brought her wildflowers when he came to the Drummond house for dinner. He bought her lemon drops whenever he took her into the mercantile, knowing it was her favorite. He had given Mrs. Tanner a deposit of money with which Lou Lou could choose some suede to have several riding skirts made. She, Dixie, and Alice would each need appropriate riding skirts when they began working on the ranch.

He paid attention when she mentioned something was of interest to her and would surprise her with it the next time he came to escort her to dinner at the restaurant or the hotel. He was amazingly attentive to her wishes. He was easy to talk to and shared everything about himself with ease. Although he and his older brother, Henry, teased their younger brother, Oliver, without mercy, Albert was very kind and respectful to Lou Lou.

She shared her untold secrets with him cautiously at first, but he never turned tail or judged her life. If anything he expressed that he considered her even more precious to him with each grain of knowledge he gained about her life prior to coming to Gunther City. Her heart pounded at the thought of him, and he seemed equally crazy about her.

Absolutely nothing stood in their way to declare their desire to be married. Minnie Smith and Samuel Knight were, ironically, the first couple to walk the aisle. Dixie and Oliver surprised everyone with an impromptu wedding right after Minnie and Samuel left for their honeymoon in the Gunther Hotel.

The next day was a Monday and Albert had remained at the ranch. Lou Lou took advantage of his absence and got some personal chores done. Laundry was her first priority. It, of course, took all day and by evening, she was ironing and putting things away. She fell into bed exhausted. The next morning, Albert did not show when the other grooms came to call at ten o'clock, so she sat in the parlor and took care of some mending. By noon, she helped with lunch preparations, even though it wasn't her day, and cleaned up afterwards, also.

Looking out the front windows from time to time, she began to wonder where her Albert was. He had been so attentive in coming to call. She knew he had a lot of responsibilities at the ranch, especially with preparing his mustangs for market, but he had always managed to work in a trip to town, or took her out to the ranch so he could get his chores done while spending time with her. She longed for the day when they would wed, and all this pining for him at the bride house would come to an end.

But he hadn't asked her that vital question. Could it be he was having second thoughts? She worried her bottom lip with her teeth as she stood at the window.

"Come away from the window, dear." Widow Drummond scolded. "You're going to wear your eyes out looking for that Forrest boy."

"He hasn't been here in two, no three days, Widow Drummond." Lou Lou hated the whine in her voice, but she just couldn't help herself.

"Nonsense, dear. Men folk got work to do. He'll be back to town when he has a chance to get caught up. You need to learn sooner than later, ranching needs wait for no one and nothing. Animals and crops need to be cared for no matter what else may be going on. It's not that you come second, it's just that the ranch must come first or everything else will fold under."

Lou Lou knew what the widow said was true. Still, she longed to be held in Albert's arms. To steal a kiss from him while his parents or brothers weren't looking. She just missed him so much.

A tear betrayed her stoic attempt to be fine while alone in the bride house. The truth was, she became impatient and fidgety.

"Why don't you bake something?" Widow Drummond suggested. "It's what I used to do when I waited for my husband to return from market trips."

Lou Lou begrudgingly entered the kitchen and lost her sorrows in baking the remainder of the afternoon. She made two dozen cinnamon spice muffins, two cherry pies, an apple tart, and a shoofly pie. The whole house became uncomfortably hot, but Widow Drummond didn't complain.

By evening, Lou Lou had already made three dozen biscuits for supper and had a roast with potatoes and carrots boiling on the stove when Helen and Jane Anne, who were on cook duty, came in to start preparations. They just eyed her suspiciously and took over the cooking. Lou Lou went to her room and buried her face in her pillow to cry. Why was Albert staying away? What had she done wrong?

The next morning, after breakfast was cleaned up, Lou Lou headed to the stairs to go to her room, anticipating another day of sulking and pining for Albert, but she heard a horse's whinny at the front door. She paused to consider who it might be, then padded to the door to check out the sound.

When she opened the door, her heart soared to the heavens. The black and white mustang she had named Lovely Dawn stood saddled and bridled with her reins looped once around the hitching post. She fidgeted from one foot to the other, but didn't pull away from the post. Albert stood back from the door with a gathering of wildflowers in his hand.

Lou Lou's heart skipped a beat when her eyes met Albert's, then dropped to the beautiful flowers.

"Lovely Dawn told me she missed you. I had to get her tamed so she could come see you and ask you a question."

Lou Lou giggled and tried not to jump up and down like a school girl. "She's tamed?" Her eyebrows rose high on her forehead. "Does that mean I can ride her?"

"Well, that depends." Albert grinned mischievously.

"On what?"

"On how you answer her question." Albert backed up until he stood next to the horse's long neck.

Lou Lou stepped out on the boardwalk. "Well, then, what is her question?"

Albert smirked, he turned to the horse and acted like he was listening to her whisper in his ear. He nodded and turned back to Lou Lou. "Well, since you do not speak equine, I'll have to interpret for her."

Lou Lou could hardly breathe. What was Albert up to?

"Alright, silly."

He scoffed as if offended. "Ma'am, what Lovely Dawn has to say is not silly."

Lou Lou sobered, but pursed her lips to hold in the giggle that wanted to leap from her mouth. She crossed her arms over her chest, pretending to be impatiently waiting. "My apologies, Lovely Dawn, what do you wish to ask me?"

Her eyes darted between her horse and her betrothed.

Albert leaned down once again, as if listening to the horse speak, and then lifted his eyes to meet Lou Lou's. "She would like to know something."

"Uh huh?" Lou Lou resisted tapping her foot.

"Well," Albert snatched his hat from his head and held it over his chest. "She asked me to ask you..."

Lou Lou tilted her head and watched Albert stepped back onto the boardwalk, then took a knee. She gasped and covered her gaping mouth.

"If you would do us the honor of marrying us, I mean me, and make us one big happy family?"

Lou Lou tried to be serious, but her lips quivered with the grin that betrayed her somberness. "You, me, and the horse... one big happy family?"

"Well, yeah. Until we have that house full of children you and I both want, our animals are part of our family, too."

"Albert Scott Forrest!" She giggled and stepped up to him. "You say the strangest things."

"So, what's your answer... to Lovely Dawn?"

She looked at the horse and back at Albert. "Well, you can tell Lovely Dawn, that even when we have children, she will still be our family."

Albert rose to stand. "Does that mean yes?"

She took another step, crossing the bride house threshold, and enveloped herself into his arms, pressing her head against his chest and listening to his rapid heartbeat. She arched her back to look up into his wanting eyes. "Ayah, Mr. Forrest, I will marry you."

He squeezed her firmly and lowered his lips to hers. A thrilling sensation swept through her body even though the kiss was brief and light. "You've made Lovely Dawn a very happy horse."

Lou Lou chuckled. "Just Lovely Dawn?"

He squeezed her again, almost a jostling-type hug. "No, you've made me a pretty happy fellow, too."

She smiled and opened her mouth just slightly, inviting him to kiss her again.

"Will you two get in this house!" Widow Drummond opened the door wider to draw them into the parlor. "I declare you Maine gals are the most exhibitioning brides I ever—" She swallowed hard and closed the door behind them, turning to scowl at them for a moment.

They both giggled and blushed. Widow Drummond sighed heavily. "I suppose congratulations are in order?"

Lou Lou snickered while Albert took her hands into his and held her close to his chest. "Yes ma'am. Miss Lou Lou Lee has agreed to marry me."

"And Lovely Dawn," Lou Lou added.

Albert's head whipped around to look at her. He spit a chuckle and turned back to the widow. "Yes, and the horse outside."

The widow pressed her brow, shook her head, and then nodded. "I see."

She left them to their merriment and hobbled to her rooms. They could hear her mumbling something about youngin's in love, which just made them burst out laughing all the more.

Chapter Four

They married the first of October in the newly erected church on the south side of town, and after spending two nights at the hotel, she moved into the Forrest's family home on the Rocking F Ranch. Dixie and she were now sisters-in-law, and life was becoming everything she had wished for.

Albert and his brothers soon began helping Oliver and Dixie build their house on Oliver's one hundred and sixty acres. She and Albert were next. By November, they moved their things into a three bedroom log home with a loft. It was perfectly suited for the large family they both wanted. Lou Lou's heart was so full she thought it might burst with joy. She spent her free time making rag dolls, small quilts, and knitting baby dresses.

But then, what should have been amazingly wonderful news brought her gaiety crashing at her feet. Dixie was pregnant.

Lou Lou was happy for her dear sister-in-law, of course, but disappointed that she was not yet pregnant. They had been married for nearly same amount of time. Surely, it was just a matter of time before she, too, would be announcing they were expecting a baby.

Lou Lou buried her despair with busy work, preparing the loft which would serve as a nursery after the babies were weaned. Once she had made over a dozen tiny quilts, she began making lap size ones for when her children slept upstairs.

By Christmas, Alice and Henry, Albert's oldest brother, were married and during the first break in the winter weather the men began putting in the foundation for Henry and Alice's home out north on Henry's hundred and sixty acres. All three sons would be living on their own land before spring. Much to Lou Lou's chagrin, Alice was keeping to herself before the purple crocuses peaked their heads out of the cold winter ground. By next Christmas they would have their little bundle of happiness. And yet, Lou Lou still had no news of being in a family way.

Spring blew in with high winds and pounding rains like Lou Lou had never seen before. All of the sister brides were married and there was talk of a new batch of mail-order brides coming this fall.

She stood on her wrap-around front porch, looking out over the pregnant earth, jealous of the ease at which nature reproduced. The wild mustangs she and Albert nurtured and trained were at the end of their season. A new feisty foal showed up every day, running and kicking beside its mother. Even Lovely Dawn had a new foal.

Spring calves dotted the meadow. Oliver and his brothers gathered them in a round up for castration and branding. Lou Lou and Dixie helped, although Dixie should have been keeping to herself in her home, like Alice. She boldly stood at the gate of the corral, her condition obvious in her expanded waist. She waddled about, opening and closing the gate for the calves.

Lou Lou rode a mare and helped cut the calves away from their mothers. Her Lovely Dawn had not weaned her colt yet. It broke her heart to hear the cows bawl for their calves. She knew how they felt, longing for their little ones.

Trees burst with new foliage, little beaks poked out of nests in the barn rafters and evergreen trees. Even Oliver's border collie had a litter of mixed pups last fall, sired by Mr. Darcy, Dixie's dachshund she had brought from Portland, Maine. They were such cute pups, nonetheless, now that they were half grown.

Samuel and Minnie announced she was in a family way. Even the only black couple of Gunther City, Emma and Sampson Cherry, who were supposedly barren, had a baby a few months back. If the good Lord could open her womb, why wasn't He opening Lou Lou's?

She fought the tears daily that threatened to fall. In church, she prayed for the Lord to bless her and Albert with a fruitful harvest of children. She was grateful for her wonderful husband and her beautiful life, of course, but her heart longed to hold Albert's child in her arms. What was wrong with her, that she was not with child?

Albert came in early one day and caught her crying. When she shared her concerns, he gathered her in his arms and carried her to their marriage bed. He shared his love with her with unbridled passion. The compassion in his eyes bolstered her love for him even more.

Later, he assured her that their love was enough. "Ma says all good things come in the Lord's perfect time, not in ours. Perhaps we are like Abraham and Sarah, when the time if right, he will bless us with our own Isaac. We don't want to get in hurry and bring forth an Ishmael, do we?"

Lou Lou wiped her tears and shook her head. "It just seems everyone has a child by now, except us."

He pulled her into the warmth of his embrace and kissed her head. "The Lord's not a fairy godmother flitting down to grant your wishes, Lou Lou. He's the sovereign Lord and knows when and what is in His plans for us."

Albert leaned back to meet her teary eyes. "I love you forever, Lou Lou, with or without a house full of children. You believe me when I say that, don't you? I will always love you whether you bear a child or not, it doesn't matter."

"Of course, my love," she answered, but deep in her heart, it mattered to her. It mattered a lot. Not that a child would change her love for Albert, she knew in her heart a child would only enhance her love and give them an even stronger bond.

After living her life completely alone in an orphanage, she wished for a family of her own to love and nurture, to give them what she never had. Had she done something terrible sinful in some way? Was the Lord punishing her for being such a disobedient servant to the Coy family? They were such wretched people, surely it was God who had let her escape. Why would He hold this most natural wish back from her, the only two wishes she had prayed for? He'd delivered the good

husband, why wouldn't He deliver the children?

Summer and then autumn rolled across the plains of the Rocking F Ranch, painting the forests in golden yellows, reds, and oranges. Winter would be here soon, and the land would go to sleep. Perhaps then, Lou Lou would be with child. She sighed heavily as she prepared to go to bed. Touching her flat tummy before slipping on her sleeping gown, she let her mind fancy the beginning of a swell.

Quickly, she donned the gown and crawled between the sheets. She and Albert would share their love for each other. Christmas was just two months away. Maybe for Christmas, she would know a child was in the making. She stared at the ceiling. A baby was the only thing she wanted this year. It was her Christmas wish.

When Albert joined her in bed, she snuggled close to him, tenderly kissing his cheek and then his ear. She trailed hot kisses down his neck. He moaned as he wrapped his arm around her shoulder and pulled her underneath him. His passion for her had not dwindled in the year they had been married. When he laid back and fell asleep, she laid contently enveloped in his arms, hoping their love had finally brought forth the life in her belly she had longed for.

The next day, a ranch hand rode his horse right up to Lou Lou's back door. It wasn't unusual for hands to deliver messages. Pete Forrest sent men to his sons' homes all the time to request their help with a big project. What was unusual was the hand tromped straight into her kitchen without knocking. His hat in his hand, like a worry stone, he stared at the floor.

Concern for his inappropriate behavior and the urgency implied by it filled her heart with fear. "What is it?" Lou Lou asked. "Is someone hurt?"

"Nah, Ms. Lou Lou, Mrs. Forrest wants you and Ms. Alice and Ms. Dixie to come to the big house as soon as you can. She's got a letter. From the sound of her excitement, it's an important letter, and she wants to share it with all of you." He turned to leave but turned back. "Oh, and she said, 'please stay for supper.'"

Lou Lou frowned. He had scared her to pieces. Why had he just marched into her home without knocking?

"Uh, if I may?" She stopped him from leaving.

He lifted his eyes to hers.

"Next time you have a message from my in-laws, can you please knock before you enter my home?"

His face burned with embarrassment. "Yes'um. I-I'm sorry, ma'am."

She nodded sternly, dismissing him to go tell her other sisters-in-law, but her mind raced over possibilities of what this letter could contain. Could it be more mail-order brides coming? But why would Gladys be receiving those? All her sons were married now. Could someone back home be sick or dying?

Oh dear! Lou Lou was twice as concerned. She hurried to finish the pie she had been baking. She'd set it in the window to cool and then find Albert to let him know he was expected at his parents' house for supper.

"Oh shoot!" Lou Lou rose to her tiptoes to see out her kitchen window. She should have told the hand to tell Albert. "Oh well."

She lowered to flat feet. She'd enjoy an excuse to ride out to him and tell him herself. She lifted the pie from the oven and set it on the windowsill. She'd saddle her mare to go find her husband, then come back and get the pie. Surely, if she were careful, she could cradle it in her lap while riding Lovely Dawn to her in-law's place.

She took another whiff of her pie and smiled. They're gonna love this gooseberry pie, she mused as she pulled her apron from her waist and hung it in the pantry. Before long she had her mare saddled and skipped alongside her with her boot in the stirrup to swing into the saddle. Lovely Dawn never stood still, and Lou Lou usually had Albert with her to help steady the horse or push her up in the saddle.

She cantered out into the pasture where she knew Albert was checking on the herd. They had bred for spring calves and wanted to see how many were successfully with calf and that they were healthy, heading into winter. She had learned a whistle from her younger brother-in-law, Oliver, that carried across the fields. As soon as she saw the men, she reined her mare to a halt and stiffened her legs to be as high in her saddle as possible, then gave the shrill whistle. Albert's head turned. He heard her and pulled his horse around to come meet her.

"Everything alright?" He called out as he approached her.

She giggled. "Ayah, sweet love. Your mother has something she wants to share with all of us, a letter I'm told. We are all invited for supper. So when you are done here, go to your parent's house instead of home. I'll bring you a change of clothes."

Curiosity filled his eyes and he smiled a half grin. "Huh, wonder what that could be about?"

Lou Lou shook her head and shrugged. "I have no idea, but I'm bringing a gooseberry pie."

His eyes rounded. "Yum." She kneed her mare to come alongside her husband and leaned over to kiss him. "I'll see you there, then."

He cupped the back of her head in his gloved hand and kissed her back. A devilish grin twinkled in his eyes, "You sure you don't want to meet at our house and then ride out to the folks."

He still could make her blush. She swatted his arm with the ends of her reins. "Albert!"

He shrugged innocently. "Just thought I'd ask."

He chuckled and she giggled. "You're incorrigible."

"That I am." He grabbed at her arm to pull her into him for another kiss, but her mare had skirted away from his horse, putting her out of his reach. She raised her eyebrows and reined the horse in an attempt to get back to where they were near enough to touch, but her mare wasn't having it. She shrugged as if to say, "Sorry," and then turned completely around. "I'll see you at your folks.'"

"If you insist," he teased and headed his horse back to the herd.

A warm sensation remained in her midsection as she rode back to their house to get her pie and her husband a change of clothes for when he came in. How she loved that man, and he loved her. Why on earth didn't the good Lord give them a child?

Chapter Five

Three sons and their wives gathered around the long dinner table. Alice had nearly refused to come, but the ranch hand that Gladys had sent to bring everyone in for supper had taken her a note from Gladys expressing the importance of Alice's presence and her condition would not offend anyone. It was a family-only gathering, after all. Dixie bounced a five-month-old on her knee. She and Oliver took turns holding the beautiful little girl. Her increasing weight wore Dixie out while trying to keep her entertained.

Gladys soon brought down a thick quilt and placed it on the floor beside the dining table and offered for Dixie to lay the baby down while they ate. She hesitantly accepted her suggestion. Gladys laid a rag doll and a silver rattle next to Myrtle. Her bright eyes widened as she reached for the shiny rattle. She cooed and slobbered, playing with the toy.

"She'll be fine." Gladys assured the nervous mother.

Dixie smiled and flashed a glance at Oliver. He nodded, agreeing with his mother. Dixie sighed in resolution, and turned back to her meal. Every so often she looked over at her baby contently playing by herself on the quilt. Mr. Darcy, Dixie's dachshund, had laid down next to the baby, her own personal guard or nanny, which made everyone laugh.

Lou Lou loved her niece, but fought the jealousy demons that tore at her heart all through the meal. Tears laid in wait behind her eyes, ready for the moment she could release them. She drew in a ragged breath and tried to focus on the lovely meal her mother-in-law had prepared of roast and brown gravy, with potatoes, carrots, beets, turnips, and hot rolls.

All three wives had brought desserts. Dixie brought vanilla chess pie, Alice had brought a spice cake with creamy icing, and, of course, Lou Lou's gooseberry pie. They were cut and distributed at the end of the meal. When everyone had a pie or cake slice sitting in front of them, Gladys cleared her throat.

"I don't know if you girls know this, but my sister is a nun in New York City. Her name in the church is Sister Bertrice. She has written me a letter asking for my help."

She cleared her throat again and slid glasses on her nose. Reading to herself until she got to the part she wanted to share, she began.

"We have a lovely family of five who have been orphaned in our Friendless Women's Asylum. I cared for their mother until the day the Lord took her home. Her dying wish was for me to place her children on an orphan train heading west.

"I sat by her death bed and promised her that the children would, 1. remain together, and 2. be adopted by a loving family.

"Gladys, dear sister of mine, the only way I can guarantee this family stays together is to give proof to the officials of the orphan train that they are spoken for by a specific family somewhere on their route. Please address your rancher families in your precious new town, and tell me if you know of a family I can claim for these beautiful children.

"Otherwise, I fear they will be lined up like livestock and removed one by one until they are scattered to the four winds along the Santa Fe railway.

"My heart breaks and my tears stain this page just thinking of such a thing happening to these children, as I have become very fond of them. I shall be praying to the Blessed Virgin Mary for you to find a suitable home and family who will love these children as their own, the way our mother loved us."

Gladys lowered the letter and wiped her tears. Her throat clogged with emotions. She bit her lip and closed her eyes.

Lou Lou swallowed hard. Her dessert sat untouched on the delicate plate before her. The tears that had been lying in wait sprang forth and rolled down her cheeks. She sopped at them with her napkin as her mother-in-law read the letter. The desire to jump up and announce she would take them, every one of them, had to be squashed, because she knew this was a huge decision that she and Albert needed to discuss.

Dixie and Alice sat silent, but were visibly moved by the plea for help. The men stared at their plates, unable to comment right away.

Eventually, Gladys spoke again. "She goes on with other things that are more personal, but I wanted to share this with you all. Should we ask for a town meeting? See if any of the new couples, or maybe Widow Drummond, could take the children? She certainly has the room in her boarding house, I just don't know if she has the energy for five children. If they are boys, I thought a ranch would be more suitable for them. What do y'all think?"

Lou Lou's lip trembled. She shook her head vehemently. A sense of urgency filled her heart. She didn't want anyone else in Gunther City to know they were coming on the orphan train. Deep in her heart, she knew these children were meant to be hers and Albert's.

Albert placed his hand over hers and looked at her with concern. "What is it, Lou?

She cleared her throat. "May I speak to you?"

"Of course." They excused themselves and pushed back from the table. The family sat in silence as Albert led her upstairs to the room that once was theirs.

Inside the room, Albert eased the door closed, and turned to Lou Lou. Tears poured down her face.

"Albert." She tried to control her emotions. "We should take those children."

He stared at her a moment. "But, Lou, five children all at one time, are you sure we could handle that many?"

Lou Lou lifted pleading eyes. "We—I wanted that many children and more, from the very beginning. It's just a short cut to what we discussed for our family size. Isn't that why we built a larger house than your brothers? So we could have a large family? Albert, this is what I want. Please, I know it in my heart these children were meant for us to love and nurture. I want to give these five orphans the home and love they deserve, that I never had. I... want... to be... their mother—" her words collapsed into sobs. Albert drew her against him and held her while she cried.

"This is important to you?"

She looked up into his love-filled eyes. "It's my Christmas wish, Albert."

"Well," he chuckled and stood back from her. "Than you shall have it."

She gasped. "Really?"

"Sure, I think having five boys, all at one time is a splendid idea. Aunt Sister Bertrice didn't say how old they were, but it would give us that head start on raising sons to help build this mustang trading business into a huge family success. Let's go tell ma we don't need a town meeting. She can write Aunt Sister Bertrice and give her our name for those orphans."

"Oh, Albert, thank you!" She cried tears of joy this time, but in the back of her mind rolled around the question. *What if they are five girls?* She didn't dare ask it, for fear he would then say no to this whole idea. Surely out of five children, some of them would be boys. She'd pray in the meantime that even if they were girls, once Albert saw their sweet faces and how much Lou Lou loved them, for she knew she loved them

already, he would still agree to adopting them.

December blew in with a terrible blizzard that lasted ten days. The Forrest men worked together to protect the herds from starvation and freezing. They had forged through the snow on horseback to find all of the cows and bring them to the lower meadows, so they were together, for one thing, to provide warmth between themselves, and so it was easier to feed them in the smaller area, which was near Pete and Gladys's home. When the storm passed, Albert and his brother's would separate them out to their own fields.

Lou Lou prepared their home for five children. Not knowing their ages, she prepared for little ones and bigger ones. The loft for the older children, the bedroom downstairs, next to her and Albert's room, for a nursery, and the third bedroom for the younger children under five. She couldn't imagine a baby among them, but honestly had no idea. Sister Bertrice hadn't mentioned the cause of the mother's death. Could it have been due to complications in childbirth or a disease? Only time would tell, and Lou Lou wanted to be ready no matter who they brought home.

It would take several days for Gladys's letter to reach her sister in New York City, and another several days for Sister Bertrice's response to come back, by then, it would nearly be Christmas. She hoped Sister Bertrice knew when the orphan train would be coming their way. Not that it mattered, other than Lou Lou would know when to expect them, and it would be so nice to have the children in their home by Christmas.

All four of the Forrests' homes were decorated for the holiday with a fresh-cut pine tree Pete had brought to them as a gift. Lou Lou made ornaments by painting chicken eggs, and crocheting delicate angels and snowflakes from tatting thread. Gladys gave Lou Lou and her sisters-in-law some of her most precious glass ornaments from her own collection.

Their tree was beautiful when Lou Lou finished decorating it. She wished she could have waited for the children to help, but she still had no idea when they would be coming. Everything she did was with those children in mind.

She had a ranch hand bring her three surplus bunk-house beds and had them cut down into child-size frames and the mattresses re-stuffed and sewn to a shorter length. Her sisters-in-law had already claimed the two cribs Gladys had from when Albert and Oliver were babies. If one of the children from the train was small enough to need one, Lou Lou would use wooden slats and convert one of the small child-size beds.

Albert had bought some calf's leather from the Tanners in town and had been spending long hours in the barn, making chaps in anticipation of sons. He wanted to buy new saddles, but Lou Lou insisted he wait to see what size they would need. Her husband set aside four horses, and had a fifth in mind, for the boys, in case they all were old enough to ride or learn to ride. Having been in New York City all their lives, they probably hadn't done much riding. But he told Lou Lou it would be a cinch to teach them. "Boys have a tendency to come natural to riding."

She just agreed with him, but in her heart, offense roused its ugly head. For one, girls can ride just as easily as boys, and two, they had no idea what gender these children were. She wished he wasn't so set in his head for boys.

Later, she rummaged through her own sewing scraps and set aside several ribbons for tying hair, in case there were some girls in the mix. She held the ribbons to her bosom. Her greatest fear was if they were all girls, she just didn't know if Albert would let her adopt them. If she had conceived and given birth, he would have no control over whether they were sons or daughters, but with them coming on the orphan train, it would be easy for him to reject them, opting for boys instead.

Lou Lou knew no matter what gender they were, in her heart she was attached already and would never reject them for any reason. If only she knew how to convince her husband to open his heart and mind to receiving the children no matter what.

She bowed her head and begged the Lord to give her the answer.

Gladys knocked at Lou Lou's back door. She hadn't realized her mother-in-law had ridden to their house, but she saw the mare as she hurried to the door. "Ma Forrest, come in before you freeze!"

"Thank you. Lou Lou, I have a response from my sister," she panted.

Lou Lou added a split log to her cook stove and pulled the coffee pot to the front so it would warm up faster. Her heart tripled its speed and her breath caught in her throat. "What does she say?"

"Come here, I'll show you." She sat down at the small breakfast table.

Lou Lou took down two coffee cups with trembling hands and filled them for her mother-in-law and herself.

"You want some pie?" She stalled. What she really wanted to do was grab the letter from Gladys's hands and read every word, but she knew good things came to those who wait. She forced herself to wait.

"No, dear, come see what Sister Bertrice has said."

Lou Lou eased into the chair, holding onto her cup of coffee as if it were her anchor. Gladys handed her the letter. Her eyes could hardly focus to read, but she made herself slow down and look at each handsomely scrolled word.

"My Dear Gladys,

"Praise be to the Blessed Virgin Mary and the Saints above. I am thrilled to know these precious children will be part of my own family. Albert and Lou Lou will be so very blessed by them. The next train designated for orphans will be leaving our station December seventeenth. How fitting it will arrive Christmas Day, just like our precious Son of Mary, if there are no delays. The sisters and I shall be

praying for the train's safe and trouble-free delivery of these little ones who are precious in His sight.

"You asked me many questions about the children, and I have prayed about this answer. I feel in my heart it is important that you discover many of these things you asked when you meet the children. Just as it would be if my niece-in-law had given birth to them herself. It's God's way, why should I deviate from His perfect will?

"I will tell you they are ages 10, 8, 5, 3, and six months, so you can prepare appropriate sleeping arrangements for them. They will tell you their names, as they are very personable and well mannered.

"May the Lord Bless and keep you and your new family. Give everyone my love,

"Sister Bertrice."

Lou Lou folded the letter along the already creased edge and slowly lifted her eyes to meet Gladys's. "Well," she nodded. "Now I know two children will sleep in the loft and two in the bedroom across from ours. I had set up the room next to ours as a nursery, but I wonder if I should move the baby bed into our room?"

Gladys smiled. "That's up to you, dear. With natural born children, you would still be nursing a six-month-old and would probably keep a crib near your bed. This child will have to already be weaned since...

well, since it mother has passed, and, of course, you... well, I think either way it will depend on what the child needs."

Lou Lou considered her mother-in-law's sage wisdom on the matter. "Ayah, I will leave the nursery set up, but be prepared to move the crib if the child needs me to be close."

Gladys touched Lou Lou's hand gently. "We have a little over two weeks before they will be here. I can see it in your eyes that you are ready in your heart, but I worry about Albert. He seems to have his head set on boys. Have you discussed what he might want to do if they turn out to be girls?"

Lou Lou started. How did her mother-in-law know what Albert had his head set on? Had he discussed this with her or his pa? Lou Lou had kept these concerns tucked away in her heart, for fear if she uttered a word, it would cause the adoption to go awry. Huge tears pooled in her eyes and rolled down her cheeks before she could get ahold of herself. "I don't know, Ma. I love these children already, just as if I had carried each one of them and give birth to them. I know Albert is set on sons, but he has said if they were ours, by birth, he would have no control over their gender. I'm praying he will remember his own words if they are all girls."

Lou Lou hiccupped.

Sincere concern shone in Gladys's eyes. "Aw, my dear Lou Lou. Albert is a kind and gentle soul. I'm sure you and he will come to terms if these children are not what he's expecting. Besides, they are arriving Christmas Day. It's a day full of surprises."

Lou Lou smiled at her mother-in-law, but in her heart she feared that very thing. If these children were too much of a surprise to Albert,

he may refuse to accept them, and then what would she do?

Lou Lou rose Christmas Day, washed and dressed as if she were going to church. Five presents sat under their lovely tree. Toy trucks

Albert had carved and assembled for the boys. She hid the individually wrapped ribbons in her dresser, just in case they were the more appropriate gifts.

She gathered one of the small quilts she had made for the six-month-old, who might be seven months by now. She had no idea when any of their birthdays were. A hollow sensation gnawed at her stomach. She knew nothing about any of them, except their age. Why did Aunt Sister Bertrice insist on being so mysterious?

Gladys and some ladies in town gave Lou Lou a nice stack of cloths for diapers and safety pins to keep them on the child. She had packed a carpet bag with several of them and a thick oil-soaked pouch to put the soiled ones in until they were back home. Dixie gave her a quick lesson on how to diaper a baby, and told her about the oil-soaked pouch for travel.

Back in Portland, Lou Lou had helped with the younger children, but never the babies. They were kept separate from the children three and younger. Other than Dixie's little girl, Lou Lou was at a loss on caring for this six-month-old who was about to become her child.

Gladys offered to go with Lou Lou and Albert when they met the train. Lou Lou accepted her offer happily. That many children surely needed an extra set of eyes and an experienced grandma just to be sure they were safe in the wagon on their ride back to the Rocking F Ranch. Plus, Lou Lou knew Gladys would know how to handle the baby's needs, if Lou Lou didn't.

Dixie had suggested they take a picnic basket with sandwiches and small cakes, in case the children were hungry. Foods that were easily held with small hands, such as biscuits, sliced cheese, and lightly steamed carrots for the baby. Alice suggested she take extra quilts, in case the children were tired and wanted to lie down in the wagon.

Lou Lou thanked the Lord for her mother- and sisters-in-law who knew exactly how to prepare for this amazing new adventure. She didn't want to appear unqualified as a mother, like the women who came to the orphanage. They would last a few days and then be long gone. She and her foster sisters could spot an unskilled helper the minute she arrived. Lou Lou didn't want these children to detect her inexperience.

As Albert turned the mule onto Main Street, they heard the train's whistle far down the tracks. It was near. Lou Lou touched Albert's arm and took Gladys's hand. Excitement filled her chest, she could hardly breathe. Her gaze remained on the pillar of steam filling the air as the train approached the depot. She released her husband and mother-in-law to fold and refold the small quint in her lap. The carpet bag sat between her boots, she looked down at it and mentally checked off the contents. She prayed she had everything she needed for the baby.

Silence settled among them as Albert pulled the wagon alongside the ticket office and set the brake. He turned to look at Lou Lou. She nodded and pursed her lips. Gladys squeezed Lou Lou's hand and stood.

"Merry Christmas, you two." She smiled. "Let's go get those children."

A tear moistened Lou Lou's eyes as she climbed down with Albert's assistance. She drew in a deep breath and turned to stare at the train's passenger car. There was no sign of the children. The coal man climbed out of the engine and straddled between the coal box and the coal car, shoveling with all his might to fill their supply. Another man pulled a rope to swing the water spout over to the engine to fill the reservoir for steam.

Albert put his arm around Lou Lou's shoulder and Gladys walked at Lou Lou's other side. They approached the platform anticipating the door opening and five children running out to greet their new parents.

When the door finally opened with a loud clink, Lou Lou held her breath. A steward walked down the steps. "Are you the Forrests?"

He glanced at an envelope in his white gloved hand.

"Yes," Albert answered him. Lou Lou opened her mouth to speak, but found her voice had abandoned her.

"Just one moment, Mr. Forrest, Mrs. Forrest." The steward tipped his hat and returned to the passenger car. Lou Lou and Gladys watched through the windows as his blue uniform passed through the car and exited through the opposite end. A baby's cry could be heard approaching as the steward led two forms back to where he had re-entered the car. Lou Lou could see muted colors of their clothes, but not whether it was shirts or dresses, from her angle on the ground, the two smaller children must be following but couldn't be seen at all. The taller child, presumably the oldest, carried a bundle.

The door clicked open and the steward held it.

Lou Lou's heart pounded against her ribs. She stared at the upper platform, anticipating the first child to come out. She sat down the carpet bag and moved toward the steps.

Chapter Six 

A red-headed girl with a baby on her hip emerged. She stayed on the platform and gestured for the others to come out. Three additional girls clustered on the outer platform, all with the same bright red colored hair. The oldest with the baby gently pushed them to move down the steps. The three year old was small and appeared to be terrified of the stairs.

Lou Lou sighed an anxious breath and reached up to help the smaller girl down. She took the five year old's hand, too, and guided them both to the ground.

It was easy to tell their age order, their stair-step heights spoke volumes. Gladys took the hands of the two who Lou Lou had guided down, so Lou Lou could take the seven year old's hand and guide her down, too. She marveled at their beautiful red hair.

Lou Lou reached back for the oldest, but she gave such an independent glare, Lou Lou backed off, and just watched in case she stumbled while coming down the steps.

The girls immediately clustered back against their oldest sister's skirts. The baby wore a long dress and a thin bonnet. Wisps of that same red hair peeked out the front and the back of the bonnet. It had no ruffle, but still it was impossible to tell if the child was a boy or girl. The older girls were clean, their boots were polished, and each wore a ribbon in their hair. The oldest stood emotionless with her chin held high. The others looked terrified and on the verge of crying. Even the baby appeared to be uncertain and clung to the oldest's neck.

Lou Lou reached out to take the baby, but the eldest sister turned slightly to pull back from her outstretched hands. Lou Lou hesitated, then stepped back. She glanced at her mother-in-law for help.

"Well, Merry Christmas, girls!" Gladys said with as much enthusiasm as she could muster. She shot a glance at her son to see his reaction.

Albert stood, gaping mouth, and staring at the girls, unable to move or speak.

The steward followed the oldest child down the stairs and handed Albert the envelope he had been holding. "Everything you need is in this, I am told, sir."

He tilted his head in a quasi-salute of farewell and re-entered the train. The girls' eyes followed his ascent as if longing for the only person who was not a stranger to them.

Lou Lou's heart broke for the fear in their eyes. Albert opened the envelope and read to himself.

Gladys peeked over his arm to see what was written. "What is it, son?"

"These are the papers to accompany the... girls." He swallowed. "And a letter from Aunt Sister Bertrice."

"Oh." Gladys rose on her tiptoes to see the letter from her sister.

Albert just handed it to her and lifted his eyes to the children. "It says you will introduce yourselves."

The oldest girl nodded and pushed her sisters away from her skirts, lining them up in age order next to her. When they were fairly straight, she curtsied, and the others did the same while watching her closely.

"My name is Magan Jervis, I am ten years old." She turned to look at the girl next to her.

She stood straight, as if drawn up to attention and curtsied. "My name is Agnes Jervis, I am eight years old."

The next girl curtsied. "My name... my name is..." She turned to her older sister and a tear rolled down her cheek.

Lou Lou wanted to kneel and take her in her arms to give comfort, but she forced herself to wait. They had obviously rehearsed this introduction.

Agnes nodded encouragement and the girl turned back to the Forrests. "My name is Edith, I am five." She held up her little hand to show five fingers. She nudged the next girl. She curtsied and spoke. "I Ryann. I tree." She held up two fingers. Then Magan bounced the baby on her hip. "And this is Baby Tipper. He was seven months old yesterday." The words clotted in her throat as emotion swallowed her ability to speak clearly.

Lou Lou gasped and turned a hopeful gaze to her husband to see his expression. So the baby was a boy. Albert's face only registered shock. Perhaps the child's gender had not sunk in yet.

"The baby is a boy," she muttered to him, searching for a positive reaction.

She had held herself back as long as she could stand. She opened her arms to the girls. The three younger ones rushed to her. She hugged them soundly. "We are the Forrests. I'm Lou Lou, but—but you can call me ma, or mom, momma if you prefer. This is my husband Albert, your pa. And that there is your grandma, Gladys. She is Sister Bertrice's sister."

The girls' eyes widened as they turned their gaze to Gladys.

Lou Lou continued, "We have everything ready for you at home. Are you hungry? We have sandwiches and soft food for the baby."

She lifted her eyes to Magan. "May I?" Lou Lou reached out to take the baby. Magan hesitated, but then let Lou Lou take him from her. He instantly leaned away from Lou Lou and wailed for Magan. Lou Lou shh'd him and bounced him on her hip.

Magan's eyes rounded and tears filled her eyes for the first time. "He's only used to me," she said and pulled the baby back into her arms. He quieted instantly.

Lou Lou let her take Baby Tipper, then folded her hands over her heart. "I'm sorry. I didn't mean to make him cry."

"He don't know you." Magan pressed her cheek against the baby's and whispered in his ear. She swayed with him as if it were an old habit. "But some food would be nice."

Albert stared at the girls then walked over to where the stewards had placed their meager bags. He lifted them under each arm and one in each hand, and took a step toward their wagon.

"Uh, food's in the wagon." He said in a gruff voice that Lou Lou had never heard. She glanced at him and gathered the girls in front of her to guide them to the wagon. Gladys gestured for Magan to follow Lou Lou. Albert opened the back of the wagon bed and lifted the girls in, one by one. Lou Lou joined them, much to Albert's surprise. He helped his mother up on the bench and he sat beside her.

Albert slapped the mule's back and the wagon lunged forward, while Lou Lou sat behind the bench and opened the picnic basket. She handed Magan a steamed carrot for the baby. He greedily gnawed and chewed on it, squishing it between his tiny fingers. Lou Lou smiled at his voracious appetite. She then handed the girls a small cake, which they giggled and ate hastily. Then Lou Lou handed them half a sandwich. When they ate it, she gave them the other half. She passed around a mason jar of water. The girls washed down their food with the cool water. Even Magan ate as if she had not had much to eat for days.

Lou Lou looked at her with concern. "You *did* have plenty of food on the train, didn't you?"

Magan blushed. "Ayah, ma'am."

Lou Lou chuckled. "You eat as though you are famished."

Magan drew her eyebrows together. "What is famished?"

Lou Lou smiled. "Starving."

"Oh, no ma'am, we are not starving. We just appreciate food that is given to us."

Lou Lou nodded. She still wondered whether they had rationed food these last ten days on the train.

Ryann stood and Lou Lou grabbed her arm to steady her. "Be careful!"

The girl stopped, then took a hesitant step toward Lou Lou, turned and sat down in her lap. Lou Lou looked at the back of her head for a moment, and then put her arm around the child. Edith scooted closer to Lou Lou's side. Agnes and Magan stayed where they had been put, while Baby Tipper fell asleep on Magan's shoulder.

Lou Lou looked around and pulled out the quilts she had brought. She laid them out for her and the girls.

"Here," she said to Magan. "You can lay him down, if you'd like."

Magan shook her head. "I'll just hold him, ma'am."

Edith and Ryann both felt heavy. Lou Lou bent her neck to look into their faces to find they had both fallen asleep. She eased little Ryann down to the quilt and then Edith. Soon Agnes's eyes closed and opened slowly. Lou Lou patted the quilt. Agnes leaned forward and lay on her tummy, tucking her arm under her head like a pillow. Magan resisted the swaying of the wagon but soon it lulled her to sleep. She gave up and laid Baby Tipper down and then curled up around him next to her sister Agnes.

Lou Lou smiled at the five of them soundly sleeping on the quilts. Thank goodness Alice had suggested they bring them.

Gladys turned on the bench to find all five children sleeping. She whispered to Lou Lou, "Looks like you're off to a good start."

Lou Lou smiled, but she felt as lost and uncertain as could be.

"Take me home, son. You all need time to get acquainted and you don't need me in the way."

"Ma," Albert glanced over his shoulder at Lou Lou and the children. "Are you sure you don't want to stay?"

"No, dear. You and Lou Lou need your own time to get to know these precious girls... and boy, without me. I'll have my time later."

"Yes ma'am." Albert steered the mule toward the main house and kissed his mother's cheek, then helped her down. He climbed back onto the bench and slapped the mule's back with the reins.

Chapter Seven

"We're home." Lou Lou gently shook the children to wake them and moved to the end of the wagon to accept Albert's help down. She held her hands up to receive the sleepy girls and lower them to the ground. They rubbed their eyes and turned to see the house. Smiles donned their faces, except for Magan. She seemed to be determined to not show any emotion. Lou Lou understood. When she was an orphan nothing was ever permanent.

"This is our home." Lou Lou placed her hand on Magan's shoulder, but she twisted slightly to move out of her touch. Lou Lou pursed her lips. This was going to take time.

Ryann and Edith ran onto the porch clapping their hands and jumping up and down. Their boots clomped on the wooden slats. Lou Lou laughed as she joined them on the porch.

"It's beautiful!" The youngest girls exclaimed, twirling around.

Lou Lou had tied evergreen branches together to droop on the hand rail along the veranda and tied red bows every five feet. "If you think that's festive, wait until you see the Christmas tree."

Albert opened the front door and the girls filed in. The sound of shuffling boots filled the room as they walked in. They stared at the tree with open mouths. Even Magan's eyes were wide.

"Can we open the presents?" Edith asked.

"Just a moment." Lou Lou ran to her room and took out the ribbons she had wrapped. The gifts under the tree were intended for boys. She hoped they understood. She grabbed the lap quilts she had made and quickly rolled them up and tied each with ribbons from her scraps box. Balancing these in her arms, she hurried back to the parlor and quickly placed them under the tree. "It seems ole Santa put some of your gifts in the wrong room."

Blank stares met her comment. She chuckled. "Go ahead."

The girls rushed the tree looking at the gifts. Agnes stepped back with tears in her eyes. "There's no names."

Lou Lou started and glanced at Albert.

He squatted next to the tree. "We didn't know your names until today, but let me see if I can figure out which is for who."

He lifted a box, knowing the trucks were all the same. He shook it slightly and placed it next to his ear, like he was listening to the content. "This one tells me... it's for you." He handed it to Magan. She handed her baby brother to Agnes and took the gift.

Lou Lou's arms ached to hold the baby. Agnes sat on the floor with him in her lap and watched Magan open her gift. For the first time Magan exhibited enthusiasm as she tore into the brown paper.

When she opened the box and saw the wooden wagon, she paused. Glancing up to glare at Lou Lou, she mumbled. "It's a wagon."

Lou Lou felt the heat of embarrassment fill her face. "Albert made it himself." She sighed.

"Here, open this." She handed her the wrapped ribbon.

Apprehensively Magan opened it. Her eyes widened when she saw the shiny ribbon. She held it gingerly in her hand and nodded. "I get it. You didn't know we were girls... except for Baby Tipper."

Lou Lou gave the astute child a small grin. "Guilty. We didn't know anything about you except your ages. Please forgive us for not knowing. We'll do better next time, now that we know each of you better."

Magan nodded, but it was obvious she pondered Lou Lou's words. She turned to her sister and took Baby Tipper into her lap. "Go ahead, please give my sisters their gifts."

Albert stood. Lou Lou watched his indecisive sway, and then he strode from the house. All the girls watched him leave. Magan turned to Lou Lou. "Did I make him mad?"

Lou Lou dropped her eyes from the door her husband had closed behind him to Magan.

"I don't believe so... No, of course not. He just... needed to see to the mule and put away the wagon." In truth, she had no idea why he had left the house. Was he angry that Magan had commented about their gifts? "Go ahead, Agnes. Open this one and this, too. Oh and these quilts are for each of you."

Lou Lou distributed the gifts among the girls, and gave Magan one of the presents which held a wooden wagon for Baby Tipper. That left an extra ribbon since he was a boy. She gave it to Magan, with an apologetic grin.

They ripped the paper and unveiled their wooden trucks and ribbons, and pulled the ribbon off the quilts. They squeezed the quilts to their chests and began playing with the trucks. Ryann wrapped her wagon in the quilt and rocked it like a baby.

Lou Lou's heart broke for them. This scene before her took her back to those shallow Christmases of her own childhood. She remembered how it was to receive charity gifts that didn't match her wants or needs, but being grateful to receive anything. Mentally she vowed next Christmas would be much more personal for the children.

Albert strode back just as Magan opened Baby Tipper's wagon. When they heard the door open, the girls turned to look at him. He held a load of folded leather, stacked to his shoulders. "Looks like Santa left gifts all over the place for you girls."

Lou Lou smiled at him. Perhaps he was getting over his shock of them being four girls. He knelt down and handed each girl the folded leather. Magan stood and unfolded it to find chaps. She wrapped them around her waist and looked up in confusion. "Is this an apron?"

"They are chaps... for when you ride." Albert offered. "And... I've got something else out in the barn for you. When you're ready, we can go out at have a look."

The girls jumped up giggling and clapping their hands. Magan stood with the baby on her hip and followed the girls out to the barn.

Albert had bridled the four horses he had chosen for the sons he thought were coming and tied them to a center pole. He led the girls into the barn and turned as if to present the four horses. "Here you are. These I chose for you."

Magan's mouth dropped open as she shied back behind Lou Lou. Agnes wrinkled her nose in disgust. "It stinks in here."

Edith and Ryann stood still, their eyes wide as saucers.

Albert looked to Lou Lou and back at the girls.

It was Agnes who broke the silence. "We don't know how to ride a horse."

Albert hesitated. "We thought that might be the case, you being from New York City and all. But I will teach you."

Edith and Ryann's faces brightened. "Really?"

Magan stayed behind Lou Lou.

Agnes walked up closer to the chestnut and slowly reached out to touch his nose. "It's so soft."

Edith walked up to the bay and touched his nose. "Oooo it is." She giggled.

Ryann stayed back but her eyes told of her excitement to have a beast of her own.

Just then, Magan cleared her throat. "Uh, excuse me, but Baby Tipper needs changed and I think I'm allergic to all this... hay."

She faked a sneeze.

Lou Lou turned to find her cowered back against the barn door. "Don't be afraid, Magan. Albert and I will teach you how to ride."

"I'm not afraid! Baby Tipper needs changed." She turned on her heels and ran back toward the house.

Lou Lou followed her with a glance over her shoulder at Albert. A shrug signaled to him she didn't know why Magan reacted so strongly. "Magan, wait up."

Magan was on the porch waiting for Lou Lou to open the front door. "Magan, honey, this is your home now. You can open the door and go in or out whenever you like."

Magan glared scornfully and continued to wait for Lou Lou to open the door. She stomped into the house and laid Baby Tipper on the quilt he had received for Christmas and proceeded to change his diaper. Lou Lou handed her a clean cloth and took the soiled one from her. "You know. I can do this now. You don't have to do everything for him anymore."

Crocodile tears formed in Magan's eyes, but didn't fall. "He's used to me doing it for him."

"Ayah, honey, I know, but he needs to get used to *me* doing things for him." Lou Lou tried to be gentle with her words.

Magan finished, pulled down Baby Tipper's dress, and lifted him to her hip. "He don't know you."

"Magan, I know. I want him to get to know me. I want all of you to get to know me, and I to get to know you. Please let me." She put her hands out to take Tipper. Magan pulled him back from her, then moved her baby brother toward Lou Lou so she could take him. The baby, having a fresh diaper and a nap, laughed and patted Lou Lou's face.

Lou Lou bounced him slightly. "You're a fine little fellow, aren't

you?"

Evening followed soon after the new family ate a Christmas dinner of ham, mashed potatoes, green beans, glazed carrots, corn, and cat-head rolls. Lou Lou held Baby Tipper on her lap and fed him from her plate. He fell asleep against her bosom. The girls yawned at the table. Lou Lou knew they had to be exhausted. "Girls, why don't you let Albert and I clean up from supper? Come on, let me show you where you will sleep."

Grateful nods answered her. She laid down her napkin. "Let me put Baby Tipper down and I'll show you your beds."

The girls clustered in the parlor as she took Tipper to the nursery next to Lou Lou's bedroom, then she lead Magan, and Agnes to the loft. "You may pick which bed you want. I'll be back to tuck you in."

Albert had already put their carpet bags in the loft so they would have their clothes. Lou Lou led Edith and Ryann to the room across from her and Albert's with the smaller beds she had asked the hands to cut down to size. "This is your room, Edith and Ryann, and Baby Tipper is sleeping in that room across the hall. He'll be closer to me and I can tend to him in the night."

Ryann looked around as if the walls were closing in on her and began bawling. Edith's lip quivered.

"What's wrong?" Lou Lou took the girls into her arms. "What do you need?"

Ryann wailed. "I sleep wif sissies."

"But, honey, they're older and can sleep in the loft." Lou Lou tried to explain.

Ryann cried all the harder, shaking her head and Edith's tears spilled down her face.

"She's not used to sleeping alone." Magan's voice from the door startled Lou Lou. She had on a white sleeping gown with a tiny blue ribbon tied at her neck and was barefoot. "Come on Ryann, Edith, you can sleep with us."

Lou Lou felt a tinge of anger at Magan for overriding her decision to separate the girls by age, but when Ryann instantly stopped crying as she took her oldest sister's hand, Lou Lou decided to let it go for now. Perhaps tomorrow, she'd have Magan and Agnes sleep upstairs and let Edith and Ryann sleep down here. She followed the girls to the ladder that lead to the loft.

"Please be careful." She watched them ascend, then followed to tell them all good night.

She sat on Agnes's bed as Magan helped Ryann change into a sleeping gown. The girls knelt next to their beds and prayed a sweet prayer. They chanted in a sing-song manner, obviously they had been saying these words for quite some time. They thanked God for their new home and they asked Him to bless the Forrests for taking them in. When they prayed for God to take good care of their momma, Lou Lou swallowed her tears. At least these girls had known their mother, unlike herself who was dropped off at the orphanage's stoop late one night.

When they concluded and said, "Amen." Lou Lou said it, too. They crawled into their beds, two in each bed, and Lou Lou pulled their covers to their chins. She kissed their foreheads, even Magan didn't pull away, but closed her eyes, as Lou Lou leaned over and gently brushed her fly-away curls to kiss her worried brow. "Sleep well, Magan."

Lou Lou paused briefly to treasure the moment. Four little girls laid in two small beds in the loft she and Albert had built just for this purpose. And now, they had five. Lou Lou sighed and gingerly climbed down the ladder.

Albert had remained in the kitchen and started washing dishes. She put on her apron and dried as he washed. They cleared away the food, placing it in jars to store in the root cellar.

"Maybe it's time we get us one of those ice boxes." Albert spoke as he came back into the kitchen from putting the jars away.

Lou Lou sat at the table, with her head resting on her hand. She smiled a weary smile. "That's a good idea."

He kissed her forehead and pulled her to her feet.

Wrapped in his arms, she felt a surge of electricity that he always stirred in her body, but exhaustion replaced passion. She kissed his lips tenderly and he kissed her back.

Albert held her firmly against his chest. "Why don't you go get ready for bed? I'm gonna finish up a few things in the barn and I'll be there soon."

Disappointed, but grateful, she nodded and hung up her apron. Soon, she was dressed for bed and had just pulled the covers back to climb in. Baby Tipper whimpered. She stopped with her knee on the bed and listened. He whimpered again and then wailed. She hurried to him and lifted him from the bed. Patting his back, she bounced him. He was wet and so was his bed. She changed his diaper, noting she wasn't as deft at it as Magan, but she'd get the hang of it soon enough. With the baby still crying in her arms, she pulled his wet linens and put fresh ones down, then rushed to the kitchen to fix him a bottle. She had fresh goat's milk and a glass baby bottle Albert had bought at the mercantile.

How hot should she let the milk get before giving it to the baby? She watched for the first bubble to tell her the water was about to boil. The glass bottle clattered as more bubbles rose in the pan. She pulled it from the stove and lifted the bottle. It was hot to the touch. Baby Tipper screamed upon seeing the bottle but Lou Lou knew it was too hot. She removed the nipple and blew on the milk as the baby pawed at the bottle, causing her to spill it all over her hand. "No, no." She fussed at him. "It's too hot."

He screamed all the louder, little teardrops oozed from his eyelashes, and Lou Lou cringed. She didn't want Magan to hear her baby brother crying and come take over. "Shhh." She bounced him and blew on the milk. Tears rolled down her cheeks, too.

Chapter Eight

Lou Lou bounced Baby Tipper against her shoulder as she fidgeted with the nipple to get it screwed on to the bottle. She leaned him back and placed the nipple in his eager mouth. Meanwhile she paced back and forth, bouncing the baby and trying to calm him with tender words. She carried him to the parlor and sat in her rocking chair, laying him on her lap, he settled and sucked vigorously.

She rocked, he sucked on the bottle, and the two of them nearly fell asleep. Soon he grew heavier in her arms and she opened her eyes to find him sound asleep. She carried him to his bed and kissed him goodnight.

Albert had already laid down in bed, gently snoring. She slipped in next to him and instantly fell asleep. What seemed like seconds later, the baby cried again. She hurried to him. He was wet. She changed his diaper and carried him into the parlor. Bleary eyed she looked at the pendulum clock. It was barely midnight. She prepared another bottle for him and paced the floor while he cried on her shoulder. Soon the bottle was warm, not too hot, and she carried it and him to the parlor where she sat in her rocker.

Ryann peeked over the pony wall of the loft. Lou Lou smiled and motioned for her to come on down. She crawled into Lou Lou's lap. She held Ryann on her left side and Baby Tipper on her right. With her left arm around Ryann, she held Tipper's bottle to his mouth. He held it himself while vigorously sucking at it. Soon she realized she could support it with her right hand that was wrapped around the baby, just so he didn't drop it, and actually put her left hand on Ryann's shoulder as she slept against Lou Lou's shoulder.

She rocked them both. The motion was as soothing to her as it was the two in her lap. The baby drank the last of the goat's milk and continued to suck air which made a noise that awakened Lou Lou. He began to cry.

Lou Lou moved her left arm out from behind Ryann so she could reposition Tipper over her shoulder and pat his back. Perhaps he needed to burp. Ryann woke with the jostling. She looked around the room and at Lou Lou with fearful eyes and began to cry, also. Lou Lou shh'd them both and continued to rock. Ryann settled down but Tipper continued to cry. Soon Edith and Agnes came down the ladder, rubbing their eyes.

"We were scared." Agnes spoke for them both.

Lou Lou juggled the two young ones in her lap to try to touch the two at her side. "It's alright. There's nothing to be afraid of. I'm here." The baby let out a loud burp, lifted his head, startled by his own noise, looked Lou Lou in the eyes and began wailing again. This started Ryann's crying again, and the other two joined in. Lou Lou looked around the room, hoping Albert would hear the commotion and come help her. She could hear his muffled snores and knew he wasn't coming. She considered calling out to him, but with the children already frightened and crying she determined her yelling out for her husband would only make matters worse.

Magan descended the ladder and rushed to her sisters. She took them into her arms and held them against her ribs. She looked up at Lou Lou, who had tears rolling down her cheeks and two babies crying against her chest. "They're not used to you."

"I know that!" Lou Lou said harsher than she intended. "It doesn't take a genius to know that, Magan. You've gotta give me a chance."

Magan's resolve broke and she began to cry, too. The six of them bawled.

Lou Lou licked her lips and forced herself to calm down.

"I'm sorry." She stood with the two youngest and moved to the couch. "Please forgive me."

She patted the couch for the girls to follow. The two staggered to join Lou Lou. Magan stayed in place with her arms crossed in front of her chest, but seeing her sisters drawn to the couch with their new mother, Magan wandered over and joined them. Lou Lou gathered them to her as best she could and reached out to touch Magan, too. The two youngest cried themselves to sleep. A moment later Agnes and Edith quieted, sniffing from time to time, but the hysterical crying had at least stopped. Magan's stiff shoulder relaxed. Lou Lou looked at the eldest. She had fallen asleep, also. Lou Lou laid her head back and drifted to sleep with all five children on or near her on the couch.

Lou Lou woke to a gentle shaking of her shoulder. Albert bent over her and the children lying at her sides and in her lap. "You sleep here all night?" he whispered.

She pulled her head forward and closed her eyes against the stiffened pain. She looked down at all four girls and Baby Tipper against her chest. She breathed the words, "They were frightened."

"I see." Albert strode to the kitchen.

Lou Lou eased herself out from under the children to follow him. Baby Tipper stirred and whimpered, so she kept him on her hip as she entered the kitchen. Albert drew water from the sink pump and filled the coffee pot. Lou Lou made Tipper a bottle and re-lit the fire in the stove, all while balancing Tipper on her hip. Albert set the pot next to the warming pan for the baby's milk. "Do you suppose he still needs it heated? He's what— seven months old now?"

Tears sprang into her eyes. "I don't know. I guess I just assumed."

"I thought the girls said they had been feeding him soft foods from their plates on the train." Albert sat at the table as if he were still exhausted.

"It seems to me a baby needs milk." Lou Lou looked at him with envy. "I could have used your help last night."

He rubbed his hand down his face. "I didn't even hear you get out of bed."

"Right." She turned to test the warmth of the baby bottle. "It's going to take some getting used to by all of us."

Ryann pushed through the kitchen door, rubbing her eyes with tiny fists. "I hungry." Edith was a few steps behind her. "Me, too."

Lou Lou nodded and lifted the bottle to Baby Tipper's mouth. She moved him over to her left hip and held his bottle with her left hand while she used her right to get out the skillet. "Albert, could you go gather eggs while I start frying some bacon?"

"I was about to head out to the barn—" His eyes took in the three children in need of breakfast, then Lou Lou's pleading expression, and reconsidered. "Of course. I'll be right back." She pulled smoked bacon from the pantry and turned Tipper away from the splattering grease as she single handedly placed slices in the heated cast iron. She considered how she could make biscuits with one hand. "Girls, would you like to help?"

Their eyes lit up. "Yes ma'am."

"Okay." She gathered the flour and lard tins and placed them on the table. She pulled out her mixing bowl and other essentials. She scooped the flour, a little bit of baking soda, and salt. She took out her pastry blender and mixed the dry ingredients quickly, then added a dollop of lard. She handed it to Edith. "Push this through the lard and make it blend with the flour."

Edith did as instructed. A lot of flour spilled on the table, but Lou Lou gritted her teeth and ignored the mess. She turned back to the bacon and flipped the strips over with a two pronged fork. When she turned back to Edith, she could see she wasn't doing bad. "Let me see."

Lou Lou took the pastry blender and finished the blending. Then she poured buttermilk from a crock.

"Now comes the fun part." She smiled at the two girls and demonstrated squeezing the flour mix and buttermilk between her fingers of her one free hand. The girls giggled and dug in, squeezing the dough with their little hands.

Lou Lou turned to the bacon. Smoke rose from the pan.

"Oh no!" She lifted a dish towel to protect her hand and pushed the skillet off the hot spot on the stove and waved the smoke to see if the meat was all right. Black slivers of bacon had shriveled to an inedible strip of pork. She sighed and turned back to the girls. Their giggles stopped when they looked up at her. Fear replaced playful delight. Lou Lou looked at the dough covered little fingers. "Well, how about biscuits and ham instead of bacon?"

They nodded. Lou Lou turned the biscuit dough out onto the table and let Edith help her roll it out to cut circles and placed them in a pan with melted lard. Albert came back in with his arms against his chest. Eggs lined his arms. "A little help?"

Lou Lou chuckled and pulled out a brown bowl. "Go get the eggs, Edith." Lou Lou handed her the bowl. Just then Agnes and Magan walked into the kitchen, yawning and looking around through the smoke-filled room.

"What happened?" Magan asked as she eyed the stove.

"I burned the bacon, but it's all right. I've got ham." Lou Lou put the last circle of dough in the dark baking pan and wiped her hands on the dish towel. Baby Tipper sucked the last of the goat's milk from the bottle and tossed it down. Lou Lou fumbled to try to catch it, but it bounced off her fingertips and shattered against the wooden planked floor.

Her eyes darted to Albert with a silent plea for help. He moved to swiftly pick up the glass shards and put them in a pail for trash. Luckily, they had bought four bottles in anticipation of a baby coming on the train.

She hurried to the pantry and pulled out a cheesecloth covered shoulder ham and sliced several pieces, leaving them on the cutting board. She pumped water into the skillet and wiped it free of the burned bacon, added a scoop of lard, and placed the ham slices in with the melting lard.

Magan approached Lou Lou and reached for her brother. "Here, let me."

Lou Lou gratefully handed him to his oldest sister. "Thank you."

Albert frowned, but didn't say anything, for which Lou Lou was glad. Burning bacon and substituting ham was a waste of food, but preparing breakfast for seven, with a baby on her hip, was not something she was used to doing, and needed time to grow accustomed to.

She put the biscuits in the oven and stoked the fire. Magan and the girls sat on the bench at the table, waiting for the food to be cooked. Albert wet a dish towel and wiped biscuit dough and flour off the table. He pulled out seven plates and five cups into which he poured buttermilk. Neither he nor Lou Lou had been to the barn to milk the cows yet, so buttermilk or goat's milk was all they had for the girls.

Lou Lou placed the skillet with warmed ham at the back of the stove and pulled out her other skillet. She put a dollop of lard and let it melt before cracking all the eggs Albert had brought in. She scrambled them and added some salt. Soon she placed a slice of ham, a scoop of eggs, and a biscuit on each plate.

Lou Lou sighed with exhaustion when she sat at the table. Albert blessed the food and everyone began eating. Magan fed her baby brother from her plate, even though Albert had put one down for the boy and Lou Lou had put eggs and a biscuit on it.

Guilt riveted Lou Lou's heart for letting Magan continue to hold the baby. "Here, Magan. Thank you for helping, but I can feed Tipper now."

Magan hesitated when Lou Lou reached for him, but then let her take him. He willingly leapt into Lou Lou's arms. She pulled his plate over next to hers and began scooping a lump of eggs into his mouth with a small spoon Gladys had given her.

She spotted something and pushed his lower jaw down to see. "He's got a tooth!"

"What?" Magan looked in his mouth.

"Look, he's got a tooth." Lou Lou held his mouth open with her finger so the girls could see the little white speck pushed through the pink gum. "No wonder you were so fussy last night."

"Yeah." Magan said.

Lou Lou ran her finger over the sharp little tooth and Tipper clamped down. "Ow!" Lou Lou jerked her hand back, shaking it.

The girls laughed. Even Albert smiled and cleared his throat as he wiped his mouth with a cloth napkin to hide his mirth. Lou Lou chuckled, too. "We'll need to mix him a gum soother."

"What's that?" Agnes asked. Magan frowned.

"It's where you put a mixture of herbs: rosehip, chamomile, and cloves, in a cloth, wet it with cool water, sometimes whisky, but that just doesn't set well with me, and let the baby gnaw on it. It soothes the gums and helps with the pain of a tooth cutting through the gum."

Albert's eyes went wide. "How'd you know about this? I thought you said you didn't help with the babies, at the—"

"I've had a conversation or two with you mother." Lou Lou interrupted him before he revealed to the girls that she had once been an orphan, too.

Magan squinted her eyes and turned her head slightly. "At the... what?"

Lou Lou glared at Albert and then turned to the girls. "Never you mind. It's not important."

Magan crossed her arms over her chest. "What! You been in jail or an insane asylum?"

Lou Lou sighed. The fact that she was raised in an orphanage wasn't as bad as what Magan had conjured up in her imagination of horrible things. She resigned herself to go ahead and tell them the truth. "Girls, I never knew my mother or father. I came from an orphanage, too."

Agnes smiled. "You were an orphan, like us?"

Magan frowned. "Not *like* us! Our momma died, we don't come from an orphanage. We were in a woman's asylum 'cause our momma was sick. She gave birth to Tipper and hung on as long as she could to feed him. We weren't abandoned! Then Sister Bertrice sent us here. Said you were family to her. And we would be her nieces now."

Magan's words crumbled into a sob. Lou Lou pulled her against her side and let her cry. Agnes and Edith sniffed, but Ryann scooted into the fold and cried too, although Lou Lou wasn't sure if she knew why she cried. "Oh, my precious little girls. Sister Bertrice was right. She's Grandma Gladys's sister. With you coming here and us adopting you, you do become her nieces, and nephew. Sister Bertrice said you were a beautiful family of children, and she was right. We are so happy to have you all here with us. You were my Christmas wish."

Agnes lifted tear-stained eyes. "Really? You wished for us for Christmas?"

Lou Lou nodded. Her throat was too clogged with tears of her own to trust her voice.

"That's why there were boy gifts under the tree." Magan lifted her chin a notch.

"And boy chaps?" Agnes chimed in.

Lou Lou looked at Albert and back at the girls. "Exactly, Sister Bertrice didn't tell us you were girls. She told us it was better we learn about you once you arrived, just like... like when a child is born and you find out what gender it is and how their personality unfolds."

Edith turned to her oldest sister. "I like my wagon... and the chaps!"

Agnes's eyes rounded. "I want to learn to ride that horse, I'm naming him Bonny Lad!" She turned to Albert. "Please don't take him back."

"We won't take anything back." Albert spoke with such compassion it melted Lou Lou's heart. "Everything we gave you is yours for always, the trucks, the chaps, the horses. It's all yours."

Edith sighed with relief. Magan stiffened. "I don't—"

Lou Lou looked at her with a question in her expression. "Don't what, honey?"

"I don't want to learn to ride. Horses... scare me." Her face drained of color, even her rust colored freckles faded.

Albert nodded. "They are powerful beasts and deserve a lot of respect. You don't have to learn to ride yours today, or tomorrow, but in time, you will need to learn. You're the eldest of our children and I was hoping you would learn to help me handle the livestock."

Lou Lou looked at Albert in surprise. Did he mean that or was he just being kind? He had spoken so much about having sons to help with the ranch. Was he adjusting to the idea of four daughters instead? "That's right. We wanted a large family from the beginning of our marriage. That's why we built this house with the loft, so that we could fill it with children. Now we have... filled it... with you."

The girls looked at each other. Magan still looked as though she wasn't sure, but Agnes and Edith seemed to understand. Agnes expressed her thoughts, "So, even before you knew we were coming to live with you, you built this house... for us?"

Albert smiled. "That's right."

Agnes and Edith rushed to Lou Lou and then Albert, and hugged their necks. "Thank you."

Magan sat still, pondering everything that had been said. "So, do we gotta call you Momma and... Dad?"

Lou Lou thought about her answer. "Sweetheart, I've heard you refer to your momma but not your dad. Whatever you called them needs to stay that way. We're not replacing either of them. Here in the west, kids call their parents Ma and Pa. If it's alright with you, Albert and I can be your Ma and Pa. That way, your Momma is still your momma and your dad is the same. We'll continue to pray God takes good care of them in heaven, while we are your second parents here on earth. How's that sound?"

They nodded. Ryann was too young to understand any of it but somehow she picked up on the Ma and Pa aspect. She was the first to say it. "You my ma?"

She turned her sweet round eyes to Albert. "You my pa?"

"Ayah, honey, we are."

Chapter Nine

Albert observed Lou Lou and the girls as they worked out who would wash dishes, who would dry, and who would put them away. Albert smiled when Lou Lou, being the tallest among the females, put away, while Magan washed. Agnes stood on an up-turned bucket in order to reach the dishes to dry them. Edith ran a wet rag over the table, then joined her little sister on the floor to play with Baby Tipper.

His wife looked exhausted this morning. She had so much to do, just getting used to caring for five children, he would help her today with her morning chores. He had already gathered the eggs, so he strode to the barn and relieved the cows of their full udders. Normally, she would have been out here at daybreak to milk them. They bawled when he entered their barn. "Sorry, ole gals. Lou Lou's got her hands full this morning."

He brought the pail of milk to the spring house, ran it through the separator and put the cream in the butter churn and the milk in jars. With four girls in the house, he figured they'd go through this pretty quickly. Next he milked the nanny goats and poured it in a jar they used to distinguish goat's milk from cow's. He'd take this to the house so Lou Lou would have it for the baby.

He glanced toward their home and dipped his chin in a decisive single nod. He would order an ice box as soon as he could get into town. Save his wife from walking so far to get what she needed to feed the baby. He sat the butter churn on the porch of the spring house for Lou Lou to make later this morning. The temps were cool enough to keep it fresh but not so cold it might freeze. He pushed her rocking chair to one side and placed the churn in front of it. All she had to do was sit down and start churning.

Satisfied with the help he had been for his wife, he strode to the horse barn. Perhaps he could start the girls' lessons today. He would saddle the chestnut, being the calmest among the four horses he had chosen for the... sons he thought would be arriving. The disappointment crawled back into his thoughts. He didn't mean to be ungrateful. These children appeared to be healthy and all... it's just that he was really looking forward to having sons.

Sadness flooded his heart. Only the baby was a boy. It would be a while before Albert could teach him to work the livestock and ride a horse.

Four girls. What were the odds? Lou Lou hadn't batted an eye when the children came off the train. She took right to mothering them. Ma didn't seem affected by the number of girls versus boys, either. Oliver and Dixie had a baby girl, Henry and Alice were expecting. There was a fifty-fifty chance it would be yet another girl. Having raised three boys, Ma was probably mighty happy to have some granddaughters to spoil and sew for and cook with.

But what this ranch needed were sons. Strong, healthy sons. This Baby Tipper looked puny and frail. Hopefully Lou Lou could beef him up with nutritious food and lots of sunshine. Albert shook his head with doubt. If only she could have given him a son of their own.

No. He wouldn't lay that burden on his wife. She had been emotional enough about not having a baby. When Aunt Sister Bertrice wrote about these orphans, his wife lit up like a roman candle on the Fourth of July. Then, for them to come at Christmas. That just made them all the more magical to Lou Lou and his ma.

Albert moved six horses out of their stalls and into the corral. Satisfied with the notion of starting the girls on their lessons today, he ambled back to the house.

"Who's ready for a riding lesson?"

"Me!" Agnes and Edith both squealed. Magan paled and stared at her baby brother. "Uh. I need to help with Baby Tipper."

"Magan?" Lou Lou drew her eyebrows into a questioning expression. "I can handle Baby Tipper if you want to go learn to ride."

The girl's eyes darted from Albert to Lou Lou and to Baby Tipper. "I-I don't feel well. I'd rather stay indoors."

Lou Lou rushed to Magan's side and touched her forehead. "You're not warm. Where do you not feel well?"

"I-I just don't feel well, all right!" Magan yelled and ran to the kitchen door.

Albert and Lou Lou exchanged a look of confusion. She turned her gaze on the two girls eager to go out. "You two go on out and ride, I'll see about Magan."

"She's scared of horses." Edith mumbled.

Lou Lou glanced at Albert. "Well, she needs time to adjust. It's all right. You two go with your Pa. Magan can learn to ride when she's ready."

Albert frowned. "No need in coddling her, Lou Lou. I want her to come, too. Ryann and Baby Tipper are too small, but the three of you can begin today. Now, come on." He said sternly.

Lou Lou's smile dropped into concern. "She just needs time, Albert."

He lifted one eyebrow and shrugged one shoulder. "I know what I'm doing."

All color drained from Magan's face, but she followed her sisters to the corral. Albert led them past the horses in the corral and into the barn. He handed each of them a hay fork and opened the stall doors. "We'll start with the proper care for these animals."

The girl's eyes went wide. Albert stepped into an empty stall and demonstrated the technique for mucking out the area, then handed the hay fork to Magan. She glowered at him. He gestured to the other two for them to enter a stall and get to work. Disappointment filled their faces, but they stepped in and began sweeping the muck toward the opening. Edith muttered as she worked. "This is yuck."

Agnes pulled the hay fork through the muck as best she could. "I don't mind. If cleaning lets us ride a horse, then we'll clean first. Besides, I wouldn't want to have to stand in all this yucky stuff if I were Bonny Lad. Would you?"

Edith considered her older sister's words. "We'll get to ride?"

Albert gestured for Magan to get to work. "Yes, you'll clean and then you'll ride."

"Oh boy!" Edith worked harder and faster. Albert smiled. At least two out of three had the right idea. Magan worked slowly, almost meticulously. Albert wondered if she was taking as long as possible to delay getting near the actual animal. Why was she so afraid?

Agnes and Edith had finished. He showed them how to lay out fresh straw while Magan continued to thoroughly sweep the manure-saturated straw toward the stall door. Albert considered whether to take the two out for part two of their lesson or wait. He decided to let Magan continue to work and take the two out to learn to

saddle a horse.

He led Agnes and Edith to the corral. "Now, girls, we're gonna saddle the chestnut."

The girls squealed and jumped in place. Albert snorted a chuckle. Their enthusiasm made this as much fun for him as it was for them. He showed them where all the tack was hung and the saddles rested on two-by-four frames. He lifted one bridle and handed it to Agnes, then a guide rope and handed it to Edith. A saddle, he hefted along with a stiff but soft blanket. "Follow me, ladies."

They both eagerly ran to the railing and leapt up on the first rung.

"I wanna go first!" they began bickering.

"Whoa, there, girls." Albert chuckled. "One at a time and then we'll see about saddling two horses and letting you both ride."

Edith jumped down pouting. Albert tousled the top of her red head. "None of that. You both listen and then you'll take turns riding him." He gave them each a stern look. "Now, Agnes, come here with that bridle."

She did as asked and handed it to him. He demonstrated how to place the bit in the horse's mouth and lift the crown piece and throat latch up and around the horse's ears and head. He showed them how to confirm it was on right and the horse was as comfortable as possible. He gestured to Edith to hand him the lead rope. She hurried to him, looked at the latch at the end of the rope and the metal eye under the horse's chin, and reached up to hook the rope there. She missed, but tried again.

He let her, yet guided her hand, to fasten the rope. "Good."

She beamed with pride in her accomplishment.

"Now, the saddle is heavy, but you'll build up to where you can handle it." He assured them while placing the blanket, then the saddle on the chestnut's back. He showed them how to bring the belt under its belly and around to the buckle. "See how he inhales?"

Albert waited while the horse expanded his ribcage. As the horse exhaled, Albert pulled up firm on the belt and buckled it at its tightest point. "He tried to outwit you so you'll make the saddle loose, but you don't want it loose, believe me. You'll find your saddle hanging down on his side and yourself being dragged along with it like a rag doll."

The girls giggled.

Albert drew in a deep breath. He was pleased he had made them laugh and equally pleased he had thought of the rag doll example which they could relate to. Maybe this having daughters wasn't going to be so bad. They'd never be as strong as sons, but with good food and time working in the barn and around the ranch, they could get strong enough to be useful.

He proceeded with a short lecture about approaching a horse, which side to get on and off, and other important things they needed to know before they ever sat in the saddle. They both listened intently, still eager to begin riding. Finally, he gestured to Agnes to come close to the horse and he lifted her to where she could put her foot in the stirrup and throw her leg over the saddle. He adjusted the stirrups to match Agnes's leg length and talked to her about holding the reins and squeezing her knees.

"Don't kick him with your boots, just squeeze your knees." He encouraged her as the horse began moving forward. He took the lead rope and stepped back while the horse walked in a large circle around him, all the while instructing Agnes how to let the horse know what she wanted him to do. Soon she was trotting in the circle and stretching her legs out stiff, finding her rhythm and getting her seat.

"Good. You're getting the idea. Now, let's let your sister have a turn." Albert led the horse over near to where Edith waited anxiously. Disappointment washed over Agnes's face, but she let him pull her from the saddle and climbed on the fence to watch her sister ride.

Albert glanced into the barn to find Magan still scraping the floor of the stall.

Edith took to horseback like a duck to water. Albert gave instructions like he had Agnes, but it really wasn't necessary. "Are you sure you've never ridden before?"

Edith giggled and squealed. She obviously was a natural. From the corner of his eye he spied Magan peeking from the shadows of the barn, watching her sisters ride. She didn't make a sound or ask to have a turn. He made no indication he knew she was finished mucking out the stall or that she was watching. He agreed with his wife that the oldest needed time to adjust and overcome her fears of the horses. But she would have to learn to ride... eventually. Unlike his wife, he wouldn't coddle her fears.

After Edith rode several laps with no problems in the saddle, he turned to the darkness where he knew Magan waited. "Magan?"

Silence met his call.

"Magan, it's your turn."

Slowly she emerged from the shadows. "I don't wanna."

"Oh come on!" Edith encouraged her oldest sister. "It's so much fun."

Albert smiled at Edith. "It's more than fun. It's necessary. You've gotta learn to ride in order to help work the ranch. If you don't learn today, you're gonna have to learn tomorrow."

She lowered her eyes to the ground. "I choose tomorrow."

Disappointment filled Albert's chest. Should he let her dictate when she received riding lessons? It seemed to him he needed to exert his authority and insist she give it a try. "Now, look here. We've got him saddled and bridled. You come on over here and let me show you how it's done."

Reluctantly she dragged her feet to enter the corral. She flinched with every movement of the horse and the horse obviously sensed her absolute fear of him. His eyes went wide, framing dark brown with yellowish-whites. Albert had a bad feeling about this attempt to teach Magan to ride, but if he could just get her in the saddle and walk around a little bit at a time, surely she'd calm down and so would the chestnut.

Albert repeated his lecture about approaching the horse and getting on and off on the correct side. He showed her how to put her foot in the stirrup and hold on to the saddle horn and back of the seat. He held her waist as she tried. The horse hurrumphed and side stepped. Magan jumped away in a backward run. Fear drained all color from her face and her eyes were wide as barrel lids. "He hates me!"

Albert tsked his tongue. "No, he doesn't. He's sensing your... apprehension."

"How can I help being apprehensive?" Magan wailed. "He could kill me. One wrong step and he'd crush me!"

Albert stepped up to Magan and placed a gentle hand on her shoulder. "Magan, they are called beast of burden for a reason. They are put on this earth to do our will. You only need to learn how to exercise your authority over him."

Magan stepped back another step. "I don't want to... exercise my authority over him." She glanced at the house. "I-I need to go help with Baby Tipper."

She turned on her heels and ran to the house before Albert could physically stop her.

"Magan! Come back here!" Albert called after her.

"She's scared of horses." Agnes reminded him. "Always has been."

"Why?" Albert turned to the next oldest girl.

She just shrugged. "Can I ride some more?"

Albert hesitated, still considering how he should handle Magan's stubborn refusal, then nodded and helped Agnes into the saddle.

Much to Albert's surprise, he had fun teaching the two girls and was just as disappointed as they when he had to end the session and go take care of some other things around the ranch. Magan's behavior gnawed at his gut. She had been disrespectful, refusing to learn to ride, but on the other hand, she was a girl. Perhaps girls weren't as prone to ride as boys. He shook his head. Every woman he knew, had known all his life, rode horses. This was something Magan needed to overcome for sure. Problem was, how to help her get up in that saddle?

"Now, girls, we'll do this again tomorrow. In fact, tomorrow, we'll aim to get Magan on a horse, too. Then we'll saddle three horses and make an important decision."

"What kind of decision?" Agnes looked doubtful as her eyes met Albert's.

"Which horse you want as your own."

Both of the girls' eyes widened and they spoke quickly between themselves about which of the horses they had already hoped to have as their own. Albert chuckled at their enthusiasm and walked the chestnut back into the barn. "Now, girls, the last lesson and probably the most important thing you need to learn about a horse, is how to properly put them away after riding."

The girls nodded and hung on every word.

He showed them how to remove the saddle and blanket, brush him down, and add to his feed and water. Mentally, he considered bringing out Ryann to see how she did on a horse. Perhaps he could give Magan more chores in the barn to keep her working around the horses, perhaps that would give her a chance to get accustomed to being near them.

He questioned whether Ryann was old enough or strong enough to ride. Maybe he'd sit with her in the saddle and just let her ride with him to get the feel for being on the horse, in a year or two she'd be able to ride alone. He hoped Magan would give it a go, then he and she could ride out into the fields, let Ryann ride with him, and he could give Magan a tour of their land and livestock.

If he could get Magan to ride at all. He shook his head. She seemed pretty determined to stay away from the horses. He'd just have to see how it goes tomorrow.

"Come on, girls. Let's see what your ma..." the term gave him pause. They, too, looked up at him with surprise in their eyes. "... has for you to do today. I know she needs help with churning butter. Have you churned butter before?"

Edith smiled while Agnes looked uneasy, but they both followed him to the house. Albert pulled off his leather gloves as he entered through the kitchen door. Lou Lou sat in the rocker in the parlor with Baby Tipper asleep in her arms. She, too, was asleep, with her head back against the head rest. Magan and Ryann sat on the floor quietly playing a game with a little bouncing ball and some metal stars. It was a pleasant scene for Albert to walk in on. He turned to Agnes and Edith and put his finger to his lips, to let them know to be quiet. Their eyes moved from his to Lou Lou and their baby brother. They nodded and gingerly sat down to join Magan and Ryann. Albert smiled and turned to go back outside. He had some bulls to check on.

Chapter Ten

Lou Lou woke when Baby Tipper stirred against her chest. She opened her eyes to find the four girls on the floor a few feet away quietly playing jacks. Bright sunlight poured through the windows. How long had she slept? The morning chores had been neglected. A pang of concern cinched her heart for the poor cows who would need milking.

She considered the girls. Albert had taken them out for a riding lesson, but here they were. "How was your riding lesson?"

Agnes and Edith chattered at the same time about their experience and how tomorrow they could pick which horse would be their own, even though Agnes had already claimed and named one. Magan's face blanched as her eyes dropped to the floor. She scooped the jacks and the rubber ball and dropped them in her apron pocket without commenting on her riding lesson.

Lou Lou watched her avoidance, considering what her lack of words meant, while nodding affirmations to the other two who couldn't say enough about the morning.

"Who's hungry?"

The girls nodded and followed her into the kitchen. Lou Lou spied a jar of goat's milk and realized Albert had milked the cows and goats. She sighed relief that the animals were not suffering from her neglect.

She spread a doubled-over quilt on the kitchen floor for Tipper, but when she bent to place him on it, he began to shriek as if she'd set him on a hot stove. She quickly lifted him and held him on her left hip while she gathered the things she needed to make them cheese sandwiches, carrot sticks, and apple slices.

It was difficult to cut the carrots and apples while holding Tipper on her hip, but every time she tried to put him down, he would wail as if it hurt to be removed from her side. She didn't want to hand him off to the girls, they had spent the past several months substituting as mother for him. Magan, especially, needed the freedom to be a little girl and not an adult. Lou Lou was their mother now. She looked around for anything that might help. She spied a dish towel and got an idea.

With the baby perched on her hip, she wrapped the towel around his bottom and gathered it on her other side. Looping it and pulling it tight, she tied it in a knot. It held Tipper against her body and freed her hands to do her work. He seemed all right with it. Pleased with her solution, she set about slicing and chopping, and steaming some of the carrots and apple slices for Tipper.

Edith and Agnes continued talking about their riding lesson. How they didn't even mind mucking out the stall, or brushing the steed afterwards. Magan's face grew angrier and angrier as they spoke. Lou Lou enjoyed the girls' excitement but worried about Magan's reaction. She questioned whether she should encourage Magan to give riding a try or just let her make the move to learn to ride when she was ready.

Lou Lou decided to not push her. She seemed to be very headstrong and just needed time to face her fears at her own pace. At least she hoped that was all that was wrong.

While the children ate their lunch, Lou Lou considered how to divide up chores for the girls. What would be age appropriate for them to do? Apparently Albert already had them mucking out the horse stalls. She ran through her head all the things she did from sunup to sundown and decided Magan and Agnes could milk the cows, Edith and Ryann could gather eggs. Lou Lou would churn the cream into butter while the girls played in the yard beside the spring house.

They'd have lunch and she'd put the younger ones down for naps, Magan and Agnes could then help Albert in the barn or out in the field, while Lou Lou baked bread or washed the laundry, depending on which day it was. She'd need to discuss it with him, but surely he expected the older two to help with the livestock. Just because they were girls shouldn't stop them from working in the fields. From Agnes and Edith's reaction this morning, they would enjoy working the cattle. Magan, hopefully, would learn to enjoy it, too, alongside their *father*.

The word caused a tingle in her heart. They were parents now. She shifted Tipper in his dishtowel wrap as she cleaned up the lunch dishes and wiped down the table. Today was laundry day, she'd fill the wash caldron and light a fire in the pit out front to heat the water. Keeping Tipper wrapped on her hip was a good idea. She wouldn't have to worry about him getting burned by the fire or the hot caldron.

"You girls bring me whatever you have that needs laundering. I'll get the wash started outside."

While the girls scurried up the loft ladder, she'd go gather Baby Tippers soiled diapers and clothes and her and Albert's laundry.

The first week passed with Lou Lou and Albert tripping through parenthood with something new to learn or deal with every day. The girls gradually settled in to a routine, as did Lou Lou and Albert, but Magan always had an excuse not to ride. Agnes and Edith were eager to go out into the fields with Albert, and Ryann rode in front of his saddle as if she'd done so all her life. Magan took to milking the cows with Agnes and even stayed at the spring house until the butter was churned and pressed into molds. Lou Lou had not intended on Magan being stuck out there working. She'd visualized herself churning the butter while the girls spent the time playing and being children.

Magan seemed more comfortable staying busy with one chore or another. Anything to avoid the horses. When Lou Lou stepped away from ironing, Magan would pick up where Lou Lou had left off. She shooed Magan away when she came back, trying to encourage her to do something fun with her sisters. Lou Lou worried Magan would never get her chance to be a child.

By the end of two weeks since the girls and Baby Tipper arrived, Albert had decided they had coddled Magan enough. He stomped into the kitchen that morning before breakfast and announced Magan would learn to ride that day or else...

He never said what he meant by *or else* and Lou Lou didn't ask. She'd rather not know what Albert might have in mind if Magan didn't learn to help with the livestock and ride a horse.

Her heart ached for the terror she witnessed in Magan's eyes as Albert marched back out to the barn having commanded Magan to be out there in five minutes. Lou Lou bit her lip and nodded agreement when Magan turned to her. "You go on, now. It'll be all right."

The other girls gave empathetic smiles. It seemed everyone in the house understood Magan's fear of horses except Albert.

Albert waited impatiently at the chestnut's stall. The other two had chosen their horses which left the chestnut for Magan. It was a good choice for her, since he was the calmest of all their horses. She needed to give him a name and claim him as her horse. Perhaps that, in itself, would help Magan deal with her unfounded fears. When Magan shuffled into the barn, he nodded but waited until she stood near the stall door.

He began at the beginning as if he had not spoken to her at all about proper care for horses. He drew the horse out and demonstrated how to saddle and bridle him. Magan watch attentively, but never once reached out to touch the horse or help place anything on him.

"This is your horse." Albert said with encouragement. "He's your responsibility, now. He depends on you to take good care of him, like you've taken good care of your sisters and baby brother. This horse needs you."

Something washed over her eyes. "Me?"

She looked at the horse as if she felt sorry for him. Albert hoped that was a spark of something that would get her closer to accepting this horse and learning to ride him. "So, first thing, you need to give him a name."

Her eyes widened. "You never gave him a name?"

"Nope. Been waiting on the one of you who chose him. Your sisters chose their horses and Ryann's too young to ride alone, so that left this chestnut for you."

Magan reached up and gingerly laid her hand along the horses head. He reared his face back from her touch and Magan jumped back.

"Don't be afraid of him. He's your horse now." Albert reminded her.

Magan swallowed hard and took a step closer to him, lifted her hand to lay it along his long face. "I don't know what to name him."

The horse snorted and shifted his front feet. Magan stumbled back from him but Albert quickly caught her by the arm to prevent her from falling onto her bottom. "Well, you'll think of something. Let's take him into the corral and get you into that saddle."

Color drained from her face, but she walked with Albert as he led the chestnut out of the barn. He began again with the lecture about getting on and off from the left side, don't kick with your heels, rather squeeze with your knees, and how to hold and guide with the reins. Magan nodded. She'd heard these instructions several times, although she'd never made it past the lecture and into the horse's saddle.

The horse shifted nervously as Magan reached up to take hold of the horn. Albert cooed kind words to the horse in an attempt to keep him still. Magan flinched every time the horse moved. Albert drew in a deep breath and let it out slowly. "Let's try something different."

He led Magan and the horse over to the railed fence.

"Climb up here." He indicated the second rung.

Curious and cautious, she climbed.

"Now, step over into the stirrup and swing your leg over the saddle."

Magan looked at Albert like he'd lost his mind, but without a word of protest, she shoved her foot in the stirrup, took hold of the saddle horn, and flopped over the saddle on her belly. The horse moved away from the fence. Magan had two choices: fall or sit up. She pulled her right knee up to the saddle, slung that leg over, and sat up in the saddle. Her face was as white as the cream in the butter churn.

Albert held the lead rope, but let the chestnut walk as he desired. Neither Magan nor the horse looked comfortable. She looked as though she knew she would fall with every movement the horse made.

"Whoa." Albert said calmly, stopping the horse from walking. He adjusted the stirrups to match Magan's leg length and stepped back to let the horse and rider get acquainted. Magan sat stiffly, the chestnut walked awkwardly. Albert let them continue making their way around the corral. He remained silent, just watching the horse to be sure he didn't ram Magan into the fence rails in an attempt to get her off his back. Albert kept his eyes on Magan, as well, she remained so pale he felt concerned that she might pass out.

After a while, Magan didn't relax, neither did the horse, but they had ridden together without any harm coming to either of them. Albert decided it had been a good lesson. He would keep at it with Magan and pray that eventually she would adjust and let go of this ridiculous fear she had for the horses. "All right. Let's dismount and brush him down."

Magan's eyes went wider than before. "Ho-how do I do that?"

Albert sighed. "Same way you got on, except in reverse."

Her eyes darted all over the corral. "But... I just... sort of fell in the saddle."

"Okay, I'll help you, but eventually this is something I expect you to learn to do on your own, besides, sliding out of the saddle is the funnest part." He gave her a genuine smile, remembering when he was young and he and his brothers would race to see who could dismount the quickest.

"Yes sir." Magan said with such a morose tone. It broke Albert's heart to think she would act so militant toward him.

He held the horse still, by standing with his shoulder under his throat latch, and wrapped an arm around his long neck while guiding Magan out of the saddle. "Swing your right leg over and just ease yourself down to the ground."

She did so, but she looked like she thought the horse would take off with her flailing beside him. "It's alright, Magan. I've got him. He's not going anywhere."

She continued down until her foot touched the ground and ran backward from the steed as if she had been set free from shackles.

Albert chuckled. "You did good, today."

Magan shook her head.

"Magan, this is your horse now. Your responsibility is to be certain he has a clean stall and food and water. You have to do this every day. You understand?"

She nodded. "May I be excused?"

"Of course." Albert watched her flee to the house with his heart saddened. He had hoped the experience would be enough to start lessening her anxiety, but she seemed to be just as terrified as before. All Albert could hope for was that with time, Magan would adjust and become a decent rider. If all he would ever have were these four daughters and one son, then he was determined to teach the girls how to tend a ranch.

Chapter Eleven

The days that followed began with Magan and Agnes milking the cows, carrying the milk to the spring house and separating out the cream. Edith and Ryann gathered eggs, although Edith did most of the gathering and Ryann merely held the basket. Agnes came back into the house while Magan disappeared into the barn, where she mucked out the chestnut's stall and filled his feed bucket and pumped fresh water into the trough.

Lou Lou called for the girls, with Tipper tied to her hip, and walked to the spring house to churn butter. The girls followed her like baby chicks tagging along with a hen. The girls played jacks on the porch and tag and other yard games. Sometimes they gathered sticks and leaves and pretended to have a tea party. Lou Lou enjoyed watching them play while she worked on pumping the butter churn. Baby Tipper cooed and spoke his baby talk, while clapping his hands with the rhythm of Lou Lou's pumping the churning stick. When one arm burned from the effort, she'd stand, switch Tipper to her other side, and churn the butter with her other hand. Soon it was time for lunch and putting the two younger ones down for a nap.

Ryann laid down on the divan under her Christmas quilt, next to Lou Lou's rocking chair, where she rocked Tipper to sleep. Every time she tried to lay him down, he woke and she would end up back in the rocker, swaying as his crying waned and he fell back to sleep. She soon became accustomed to just staying in the rocker and catching a little nap herself.

Yellow-green buds filled the pecan trees near the house and bright green grasses poked up among the brown winter fields. Albert had Agnes and Edith ride out with him and two of his dad's hands to gather the expectant cows into the pasture near Albert's home. They would calf soon, and Albert didn't want them too far out where coyotes could hurt the newborns.

Agnes and Edith's horses had already been trained for working the cattle. Albert shouted instructions, but for the most part, the horses worked from trained instincts and the girls let them do what they did best. The cows lowed and bellowed as they slowly headed in the direction Albert wanted them to go. He leapt from his horse and opened a gate wide to let them into the field in which he wanted them to stay until the calves were born.

Agnes and Edith walked their horses behind the last of the cows as they all entered the designated field. Agnes leapt from her horse and closed the gate. Albert gave her an approving nod. She climbed back into her saddle and followed him and the bovine across the field. They'd leave them here and go back to the house.

Edith rode to the stock pond. Albert had instructed her to pump more water before she came in. Agnes joined her, knowing Edith would wear herself out pumping the well water. Edith had already begun lifting and lowering the lever. It took both her hands and all of her weight to pull it down, then she had to stand on the platform and pull with all her might to lift the handle. Suddenly she screamed and fell back from the pump.

Agnes turned from having just dismounted and heard the rattle.

"Snake!" she screamed, and ran to her sister's side. Edith held her right wrist with her left. Blood oozed from between her fingers. Agnes stood to her full height. "Albert! Help!"

Albert vaulted back on his horse and galloped to where the girls were. He leapt off his horse, with his hand pulling out a knife from a pocket along his pant leg. "Go to the house, get your mother."

Agnes's wild eyes darted between Edith and Albert as he knelt down beside Edith and opened his knife. "What are you gonna do?'

"I'm going to do what I can, but we'll need Doc Savage. Hurry, go tell Lou Lou."

Agnes ran to her horse, scrambled up into the saddle and kicked the horse into a full gallop without stopping until she reached the back door. "Lou Lou!" She screamed. "Ma-Mother!" Tears began to clog her voice. "It's Edith, help!"

Lou Lou shoved the screen door open. Baby Tipper hung from her hip as always. "What's happened?"

Agnes swallowed and forced herself to speak clearly. "Edith's been bit by a snake, Albert said we need Doc Savage."

Lou Lou turned to look at Magan.

Magan's eyes went wide with terror. She shook her head as she ran to the door to look out in the field at the two bodies down on the ground, near the pump. "I-I can't."

"You have to. Ride into town and get Doc Savage. Tell him Edith's been bit. I'll go help Albert bring her into the house."

Magan stared at Lou Lou as if she had no comprehension. Edith's scream echoed from the field. Magan started, as if shaken out of a trance. "I'll go."

She ran to the barn, saddled and bridled the chestnut, and tore out of the barn toward town. It was the first time she'd ridden at a gallop. Lou Lou watched her go, then turned to grab a small basket with bandages, a jar of clay, and smelling salts. She pinched off a hunk of bread and tossed it in the basket and ran, as best she could with Baby Tipper tied to her hip, out to where Albert knelt with Edith. Agnes ran with her.

Albert sat up, next to Edith. Blood ran down his chin as he spit across Edith's body. Had he been hurt, too? No, Lou Lou shook her head, he had sucked Edith's blood from the snakebite wound. Lou Lou nodded her approval. Edith looked pale as she laid unconscious. "She fainted when I cut the bite."

Lou Lou nodded. She pulled out the smelling salts and poured a small amount of the ammonia on the wound, then mixed the bread and clay together, pressing it against the bite, and wrapped it tightly with the bandages. "You pick her up and carry her to the house."

Lou Lou stepped back to let Albert get ahold of Edith. When she was in his arms, Lou Lou held the vial of smelling salts under Edith's nose. She choked as she woke and began crying. "It's all right, Edith." Lou Lou comforted and ran beside Albert, holding Tipper close to her chest so she could move more quickly.

Magan was so relieved when Albert took her two younger sisters to gather the expectant cows to the field near the house. She looked forward to watching the momma cows and seeing the newborns, but so glad she didn't have to ride out, too. So far, she'd ridden her chestnut several times, but only in the corral where he couldn't run off or throw her from the saddle.

Or trample her.

She knew why she was so terrified of the horse. It was a fear she couldn't seem to get under control. Every time the horse moved, she just knew she would be trampled like that woman she'd witnessed in the streets of New York City.

Magan had been gazing out a window when a woman crossed the street that ran in front of the asylum. The woman seemed hysterical over something, Magan had no idea what. She blindly ran out in front of a horse and carriage. The driver didn't notice the woman until his horse reared in her harness and came down square center in the frantic woman's chest. She was dead, instantly. People ran to her aid, but it was too late. Magan watched a man in a top hat watch the whole thing from the opposite walkway, but never move out to the woman. Eventually, he ducked his head and turned to walk away. Could he have been why the woman had been so distraught she didn't even see the danger she'd put herself in?

Magan feared with all her heart that if she made one wrong move, she'd be crushed under a single hoof like that woman had been. Then she'd be dead, like Momma. Sister Bertrice told her and her siblings that Momma was with God now, but Magan just didn't know. What really happened when a person died? Momma just seemed to go to sleep. How could she be with God, or anybody, if she was asleep?

Magan had stayed in the house and helped Lou Lou make five loaves of bread. They had just taken two loaves out of the oven when she heard a scream and soon Agnes's horse sliding to a halt at the back door. Agnes screamed for Lou Lou. She was out of her mind with fear, even called Lou Lou mother. None of them had called her Mother, or Albert Father. It just didn't seem right. But something was terribly wrong. And when Agnes screamed "Mother," Magan knew that something was extremely bad.

Edith!

Agnes screamed that Edith had been bit by a snake. A snake? In New York they didn't have snakes. But Albert had warned them about the rattling kind out here on the prairie. He had said they'd hear them before they'd see them. Why hadn't Edith seen it? How bad could it be? From the reaction of Lou Lou, Magan determined it had to be bad. Could Edith die from a snake bite?

Magan's heart slammed against her ribs. She couldn't lose Edith, too. When Lou Lou turned to her and told her she had to ride to town and get the doc, she knew it was what she had to do, but for the initial moment, she couldn't make her feet move. She didn't want to ride that horse beyond the corral. If she fell off, he would trample her for sure.

But Edith needed her!

She had to do it. She had to ride to town and get Doc Savage. She didn't even know who Doc Savage was, but as small as the town of Gunther City was, surely she could find him. Even if she just simply rode down the one main street and screamed out for him. Someone would point her in the right direction.

She'd only been in town once, the day they arrived on the train, but she knew the one road leaving the ranch would take her there and she remembered there was only one road down through the center that led to the train station.

She could find it.

She had to.

For Edith.

"I'll do it." Magan knew she had no choice. Lou Lou and Albert had to treat Edith's wound until the doc could get there. She'd just have to stay in that saddle and not let the horse trample her. Edith needed the doc and Magan was the only one who could go get him. She dashed past Lou Lou and slipped the bit in the chestnut's mouth and pulled it over his ears. Then she saddled Chester just as Albert had taught her.

"Come on, Chester. We've gotta get the doc." She whispered as she climbed the stall wall and jumped over into the saddle. Shoving her feet into the stirrups, she squeezed her knees quickly, rocking her bottom in the saddle, and hung on for all she was worth. She'd never ridden him while he ran, but there wasn't time for any more lessons. Edith's life depended on Magan doing this.

By the time she left the ranch from under the huge family entrance with Rocking F Ranch carved on the top logs, she could feel the horse's rhythm and her own coming together. She wasn't bouncing all over the saddle, but swaying in sync with Chester.

It dawned on her, also, that she was calling him Chester. She didn't realize she'd named him. Albert always called him the chestnut. That was his color. But today, in Magan's haste, she'd just blurted out Chester. It fit him, too. "Go, Chester," she said to her horse and leaned over his neck and let his reign lay loose in her hands. He seemed to understand the urgency and ran faster than she'd ever seen a horse run. Before long, they came into town. The blacksmith's shop was on her right and the stables were on her left. She let Chester continue to run, reading the signs that hung above the businesses. As the train depot came into sight, she looked to her right and saw a shingle swinging against the wind, "Doc Savage, MD."

She pulled Chester's reins and leaned back with them tight in her hands. Yelling as she swung her right leg over the saddle and slid to the ground. She tossed the leather straps around the hitching post and continued running. "Doc Savage! I need Doc Savage!"

A man in a Sunday suit rushed to the door and opened it wide for her before she had a chance to beat on the frame. "What is it?" the man said calmly.

"My sister's been bit by a... snake! Lou Lou and Albert Forest, they're my... parents, they're treating her, but sent me to get you."

He nodded as she spoke, as if he understood what she was saying before she said it. "Let's take your horse down to the stables and get two fresh horses."

Magan stopped in her tracks. She'd never ridden any horse except Chester. "No. I'll take Chester, you get a horse at the stables."

He hesitated, grabbed a black satchel, and put his hand on her back, pushing her out the door. "All right, we'll ride double to the stables."

She nodded and ran to her horse.

Chapter Twelve

"You did right, both of you." Doc Savage put his instruments back into his black satchel. "Albert, cutting and sucking the venom right away helped, and the ammonia followed by that bread and clay poultice drew the rest of the poison out. I had anti-venom in my stores, but I didn't have to use so much with all that you two had already done."

Lou Lou clung to Albert's side, Baby Tipper wrapped on her right hip. The doc let his eyes rove over her wrapping with interest. "She's gonna be fine. Just let her rest until she feels up to getting up. She'll let you know when she's better."

He winked at Edith and smiled at Magan, then lifted his gaze to Baby Tipper wrapped snugly to Lou Lou's hip.

"This looks like a handy system." He nodded toward Baby Tipper. "I can see where this helps you and him. I can't imagine what a baby goes through losing a momma at such a young age. I'll bet this helps him feel more secure."

Lou Lou smiled, but didn't say anything.

"Well, good thing you have so many children, Albert. It was a good thing Magan could come get me as fast as she did." The doc gathered his satchel and put his hat on his head. "I'll come check on her in a few days, in the meantime watch that wound for redness or fever. Just send Magan to get me if anything doesn't seem right." He smiled at Magan again, as if they had a special bond now.

Magan pursed her lips, but finally let a slight smile curl on one side of her mouth. "Yes sir. I can come get you if Edith don't get better."

Albert rested his hands on Magan's shoulders.

"We're real proud of you, honey," he said softly next to her ear. She looked at her sister. Edith smiled at her as she cradled her wrist in her left hand. "You rode the chestnut all the way to town?"

Magan nodded. "Yeah. Chester is a lot faster than I ever imagined."

"Chester?" Albert said.

"Yeah, it came to me when I saddled him, you always call him the chestnut, and when I needed to let him know I wasn't gonna let him trample me under his feet, I needed to call him something. It just came out Chester. It seemed to suit him and so, we stuck with that all the way to town and back again."

Albert laughed, as did the Doc.

"Well, whatever gets you in that saddle, works for me." Albert patted her shoulder. Lou Lou pulled Magan into her arms and hugged her. "You're the bravest girl I know, Magan. Thank you."

"I'd do anything to save Edith, Ma."

Lou Lou leaned back and looked into Magan's eyes, her mouth agape. "You called me Ma?"

Magan shrugged. "I figured it suited you, too."

"Well," Doc Savage touched the brim of his hat with two fingers and a thumb, "I'll be getting out of your hair now, but I'll be back in a couple of days."

"Thank you, Doc." Albert shook his hand and walked him out to the yard.

Lou Lou wrapped Magan in a tender hug again, and sat down beside Edith. "How about some soup?"

EPILOGUE

"There." Lou Lou stepped back from the Christmas tree her father-in-law had brought to each of his son's homes. "That's the most beautiful tree I've ever seen."

"Even more beautiful than last year?" Magan asked.

"Even more beautiful." Lou Lou nodded. "Because this year, you and your sisters helped make new decorations and string popcorn and made colored paper chains. This Christmas is going to be the best one yet."

Agnes laughed. "It certainly is less scary."

Lou Lou hugged her second oldest daughter. "I'm sure that's true. We had no idea what to expect, waiting for y'all to get off the train. We didn't even know you were girls, 'til we laid eyes on you."

Edith hugged Lou Lou. "I'm glad it was you waiting for us, Ma."

"I'm glad, too, Edith. You five were the best Christmas wish a momma could hope for."

Tipper toddled up to the tree and patted a branch.

"No, no, Tipper." Lou Lou lifted him onto her hip. "Don't break a glass ornament, please. Grandma Gladys would be very sad."

Ryann pulled on Lou Lou's skirt. She squatted slightly and lifted the four year old onto her other hip, and straightened with a groan. "You're getting heavy, Ryann."

"I'm a big girl." Ryann said and the other's laughed.

"Yes, you are getting to be a big girl. Soon you'll be riding horses with your sisters and rounding up cattle just like the men." Ryann laughed with the others.

Tipper took advantage of Lou Lou's distraction with Ryann and reached out to take hold of an egg ornament. Lou Lou turned her body just enough to bring him back from touching distance of the tree. "You stinker."

Albert strode across the room, wrapped an arm around his wife and the two children in her arms. "You girls did an excellent job this year."

"Thank you." Lou Lou said as she smiled at the four girls. They smiled back.

"Thanks to you," Albert said to his wife. "Because of your Christmas wish, we have a wonderful life, a family with five children and—"

"That's not quite right." Lou Lou gazed at her husband. A twinkle glistened in her eye.

Albert scanned the girls' faces. They looked up at Lou Lou with confusion in their expressions. "What do you mean?"

Lou Lou smiled, shifted Ryann on her left hip, then shifted Tipper on her right. "My original Christmas wish was to fill this home with six children."

"Well, that didn't happen, and it's all right, these children are such a blessing—"

"No, but it will." Lou Lou swept the faces and landed on Albert's. "By summer, we'll have all six."

Albert stared at his wife. "Really?"

Magan and Agnes sucked in air and began jumping up and down. Edith and Ryann laughed but weren't sure what they were excited about. Tipper laughed and swatted at a tree ornament. Lou Lou pulled him back from the tree. "Ayah, really. I'm gonna have a baby."

Edith's eyes went wide. "Oh! I hope it's a boy!"

Albert pulled his wife closer into his embrace, despite the two children in her arms. "Boy or girl, it doesn't matter. Not to me, anyway."

"You mean that?" Lou Lou looked at her husband sternly.

"One thing I've learned in this last year" —he smiled at his four daughters— "girls make mighty good ranch hands."

Magan giggled. "Once we learn to ride a horse."

The End

Love the Story?
Leave a review, please.
Next book in this series is Alice's Trebled Heart[1]

---

1. https://geni.us/Aqbjb

Notes to Reader:

Characters in the Gunther City Mail Order Brides Series are named after my own family who were among the founders of Guthrie, Oklahoma in 1889 and acquired their land holdings April 22 in the land run.

William and Mary Etta are my great-great-great grandparents. Claude and Wilma and Pete and Gladys are cousins of my grandmother.

Martha was my grandmother from this side of the family.

GW was one of my favorite 2nd cousins and he was the one who could mount a horse by running and jumping over its rump. I have dedicated this book in his memory.

Lou Lou is a cousin of mine, unrelated to the settlers.

These stories are fiction, but there are elements of the stories told to me by my Great Aunts who were there woven into each mail order bride's story.

About the Author

Lynn Donovan is an author, playwright, and director who spends her days chasing after her muses trying to get them to behave long enough to write their stories. The results are numerous novels, multi-author series, anthologies, dramatizations, and short stories.

Lynn enjoys reading and writing all kinds of fiction, historical western romance, paranormal, speculative, contemporary romance, and time travel. But you never know what her muses will come up with for a story, so you could see a novel under any given genre. All that can be said is keep your eyes open, because these muses are not sitting still for long!

Oops, there they go again...

Want more?

You can learn more about Lynn when you follow her on her Facebook Author Page at https://www.facebook.com/LynnDonovanAuthor, join her reading group on FB at Books by Author Lynn Donovan @ https://www.facebook.com/groups/BooksbyAuthorLynnDonovan/, her website LynnDonovanAuthor.com[2] and Twitter @MLynnDonovan,

For more publications by Lynn Donovan go to: Amazon.com/author/ldonovan

---

2. http://LynnDonovanAuthor.com

Appreciation

Thank you to everybody in my life who has contributed in one way or another to the writing of this book. My husband, my children, my children-in-law, and my grandchildren. You all are my unconditional fans. My BETA reader and grammar guru who make me look gooder than I am. [Bad grammar intended.] My fellow author friends who chat with me daily to exchange ideas, encourage, maintain sanity, and keep me from being a total recluse/hermit.

Mostly I thank God for the talent he has given me. I hope to hear you say, "Well done, my good and faithful servant," when I cross the Jordan and run into your arms—Many, many years from now. :).

Newsletter and a Free Gift for You

Hey! Thank you for purchasing and reading this book. I'd like to give you a parting gift to show my appreciation. Sign up for my newsletter at lynndonovanauthor.com/newsletter. I will send you an e-copy of a collection of short stories I wrote purely for your entertainment. I will happily send you this e-copy for FREE, if you ask. I will also add you to my NEWSLETTER list and you will receive up-to-date information

on new release before anyone else.

This book will **not** be sold anywhere, at any time, I am keeping it exclusively for you, my readers, and only if you ask for it.

Thank you again, and God Bless.

~Lynn Donovan